SAVAGE ELITES

ROYAL ELITE ACADEMY SERIES

M.A. LEE

Contents

CHAPTER 1

ASON

My destiny had been sealed, even before I was born.

I guess being the son of one of Savannah's most notorious mafia Capo's, Aiden Antoni, it was just expected that I would follow in his footsteps. My legacy defines me in ways that both excite and anger my soul.

I come from a family of power, wealth, and prestige. My father became a made man when he was a teenager. Not much older than what I am now—seventeen-years-old. He built an empire and has ran the Antoni Mafia Family with ease for years. I will inherit his empire and someday work for him and his crews, gaining a status and bank account that would set me up for the rest of my life.

The only problem; I don't want any of it.

Not the power.

Not the endless supply of girls that seemed to pop up everywhere I went.

Not even the money I was destined to inherit even before I was an adult.

Though, I wished more than anything that I could say those things aloud, I just couldn't.

I knew that there were men who would literally kill to be born into a powerful mafia family like mine. Even my 'uncles,' Ryder and Solly, had fought with their lives to get into our family. I knew that saying I didn't want to be part of the mafia would surely destroy my father—so that's why I shut my mouth and pretended to enjoy every moment I endured.

A slap on my shoulder jolted me from my thoughts as I stared out over the vast landscape of my house.

"Son, what are you doing?" my father asked, as he stepped out onto the porch.

His dark hair was starting to show flecks of gray, but he still looked suave and dangerous as always. His brooding personality had everyone around him trembling with fear, but I had never really been afraid of my dad. He was different with me and my mom. Gentle and loving—a stark contrast to the persona he worked so hard to obtain. But still, there was a darkness that surrounded him that on occasion, had me slightly fearing what he was capable of.

"Hey, dad. I just got home from hanging out with the guys," I replied.

I was still in my school uniform and the gentle breeze from the willow trees made the air feel nice.

"I need to talk to you," he said, glancing down at his gold watch. "I have a meeting in an hour, but your coach called me this morning," he began, his dark eyes narrowing on me.

Sighing, I ran a hand through my dark hair. I knew that I was in hot water with my coach. He knew about my skipping class lately and my dad had on more than one occasion, caught me paying other students at school to take tests for me.

"What about?" I asked, acting as though I didn't have a clue as to what could be wrong.

Dad leaned against one of the stone pillars on our back deck. "Ason, your coach was close to kicking you off the team. You are failing several classes and skipping. I had to pay for new stadium seating at the ball field to entice him to keep you on the team. Things need to change," he warned.

I heard the anger in his voice and knew he was pissed, but I didn't bother to look away from the fading sunset that lit up the evening sky. Reds, oranges, and purples were painted before me, almost like mother nature was creating a master-piece.

"Ason, do you have anything to say about this?" he asked, his tone sharp like a double-edged sword.

This time, I glanced back at my father. I knew that he thought what he was doing the best for me, but really, he was only adding to the suffocation I felt. I wish I had the nerve to tell him that I hated my preppy school and all of the assholes that filled the classes. I wanted to tell him that I didn't care about my baseball team or becoming another guy in his mafia world. I didn't, though and knew that I never would.

"I'm sorry," I said, trying to sound sincere.

My mom opened the glass French doors that led from our kitchen out onto the patio. A smile struck her face and I saw my dad soften a bit at the sight of her. They had this weird kind of love that sometimes made me sick. I guess it was the only nice thing in my life—I had parents who actually loved one another. Most men in the mafia cheated on their wives and had mistresses hidden all over the city, but not the Antoni men. They loved fiercely and with a protection that can only be described as animalistic. In their kingdoms, they are the kings and there is only room for one queen.

"Ason, you know your dad and I love you very much, right?" mom asked, glancing between me and my dad.

I knew that she could feel the tension growing between us and she hated when we fought. Unfortunately, our bickering had become a daily thing around here.

"I know, mom," I sighed. I wish they would just get off my back. This was my senior year and I just wanted to enjoy it as best as I could.

My dad pushed himself off the pillar and stood next to me. "Get up, Ason," he ordered.

This time, I didn't try to act indifferent. My dad was royally pissed and I knew that I needed to listen to him.

Standing, I stood there between my parents, watching as creases formed in their brows as they grew frustrated with me and my attitude.

"I made a call with the school. You will attend weekly tutoring sessions until your grades are passing, and that I am confident that you won't let them slip again," dad began.

"What? You can't be serious?" I almost yelled out.

Anger flooded my vision and I wanted to scream out in rebellion. Tutoring? Me? There was no way I would be forced to such shitty circumstances. We were the Elite, after all. If there was ever a time to be proud of my circumstances, this was it.

"I am very serious," dad warned.

"Ason, we won't stand back any longer and let you spiral out of control. It's time to put our foots down," mom chimed in.

I saw her eyes mist over and her bottom lip tremble. I swear, if she cried, that would be my undoing. I may be tough with a hard exterior, but I can't stand to see my mom cry.

"Can't you just pay the school again? I'm sure they could use a donation for a new gym or something," I began, but dad held up his hand to silence me.

"Ason, at some point, I have to stop throwing money at your problems. I have worked very hard to get the success I have today. I won't watch my only son throw his life away because he is spoiled."

His words cut like a knife and I winced. Spoiled? Sure, I enjoyed nice things, but I never asked for anything. And, what's the point of having money, if you don't use it?

"You will go to your tutoring session and you are suspended from the next three games. You will still attend practice and no more skipping classes," mom added, before wiping a tear away.

Shaking my head, I felt the urge to scream. My face was hot and my fists were balled up at my sides. My anger had always been one of my biggest downfalls. I had a temper and when it flared, it could get really ugly.

"This is insane," I bit out.

I didn't trust myself to say anything else.

Nodding, dad looked at mom and then she went back into the house. He stepped closer to me so that we were nose-to-nose. His dark eyes were smoldering as he stared me down. I had never feared my father until that moment. I knew what he was capable of, but I never would have thought he would hurt me...

"Listen to me, Ason. I refuse to allow my son to throw his life away. You mope around here and are wreaking havoc at school. I've built an empire that will be handed down to you one day. This life that you so carelessly dismiss is not one to be tampered with. You will do this until I am pleased," he stated.

He continued to stare me down for what felt like forever. My own stubbornness took over and I stared back at him, refusing to back down. I may not be the capo, but I was strong, nonetheless

"When do I have to start this?" I asked, though gritted teeth.

"Tomorrow. Your tutor is being notified tonight. Her name is Scarlette, I believe," he said, dismissing it.

I perked up at this. There was no way it could be *her*—could it?

I only knew of one Scarlette at my school who was a tutor and it was someone who I had claimed only in my dreams. A girl that was too good for a criminal world like mine. This was worse than I could have imagined.

Finally, dad stepped away and I listened as his shoes clicked against the concrete patio. I waited until he was gone before I exhaled a deep breath. I knew that I had been fucking up, but I didn't think it needed such extreme actions. Closing my eyes, I missed as the sun set and I cursed myself. Like it or not, I needed to get my shit together.

Chapter 2

Scarlette

When you live in a fake world, it is difficult to recognize anything real.

Take for example, my high school. At Royal Elite Academy, everyone here pretends to be someone or something they are not. We are all wealthy through our parents; of course. However, that doesn't change the way over half of the population act as though they are better than everyone around them. Walking through the halls of the prestigious private school, Royal Elite Academy, I inhale a deep breath. My nerves go wild as I hold my laptop close to my chest and adjust my backpack on my shoulder. The pristine white walls feel sterile and uninviting. The world around me feels like it is spinning out of control and I am lost in this abyss that I will never escape from.

"Hey, move," someone growls out, shoving my shoulder as they walk past me.

I mutter an, "I'm sorry," as I side-step out of the way.

It's too late, though. All I can do is watch as though in slow motion; the Elite walk past me. Gabby, Talon, Micah, and Ason glide down the hallway like they are walking on air. The girl who had pushed me, now stands beside me, her mouth opens wide as she stares their way. Everyone parts for them, no one daring to get in the way of the schools most notorious group of friends.

No one dares to speak to the Elite without being spoken to first. It's been that way forever it seems. The air around them shifts, almost growing too heavy to breathe. They are all so strikingly beautiful that it is almost painful to look at them. The hype is in full swing today since it's the first day back from Spring Break of school of our senior year. Over the break, the Elites had vacationed away from Savannah and hadn't been seen until now. Everyone speculated where they had gone—of course, together—but no one really knew where they went. It was always a secret, for their protection, I guess.

Ason turns my way, and I drop my head. Refusing to look his way, I hold my breath until I feel the crowd begin moving again. It's been this way forever. Even in kindergarten, we all recognized the difference between the real Elite and the rest of us. Yes, we were all wealthy as our families afford us the privilege of attending an elite private school in downtown Savannah, Georgia. However, there was always something different about them. Magical almost. We all felt the differences. The power they held and still hold even to this day. They run this school and we all allow it.

"Scarlette, wait up," I hear from behind me.

I turn in time to see my best friend, Macy, running down the long, white hallway. Her black heels click against the shinning floor as she hurries toward me. I stop walking and wait.

"Hey," I say, once she catches up to me.

"I saw the Elite walk past you," she says, quirking her eyebrows.

Handing me a steaming cup of coffee, Macy and I begin to walk toward our lockers. I take a sip of the liquid gold and sigh. She must have picked it up from the school coffee cart.

"Yeah, and the whole school bowed down to them," I jested, rolling my eyes.

Macy shook her head, causing her long, wavy blonde hair to sway all around her face. "Don't you ever wish you could be one of them?" she asked, smiling a little.

We opened our lockers, grabbing our books for the day. I hesitated and took much longer than needed to get all of my things organized. I hated how everyone wanted to be part of the Elite's circle. It was like a coveted society that everyone desperately desired to be part of. Only, none of us had really ever had a chance. I mean, the Ason, Talon, and Micah got any girl they wanted, but as for really being friends with them—none of us had ever stood a chance.

You had to be part of their world. A world filled with dark rumors and dangerous lifestyles. Maybe that was the real fascination with them all. They were so elusive that it made us all want a piece of them.

Well, everyone but me. While everyone around us had craved to even be talked to by the Elite, I had always kept my distance. Being popular wasn't as important to me as it was to most of my peers. I wanted to get out of Savannah and start a life far away from this world.

Shaking my head, I slammed my locker closed. "No. There is nothing about their lives that I want," I say a little too bitterly.

Macy gawks at me as she falls in stride next to me. We walk toward our first class of the day—English. She has always envied the popularity of the Elites, while I have never seen the real appeal of them. I mean, don't get me wrong. They are all beautiful, but other than that, there really isn't anything special about them.

As we walk into our classroom, we make our way down the aisles until we find our seats in the middle of the room. Sliding into my chair, I begin gathering my things for class. Macy sits down next to me and leans over.

"It's our senior year. We need to at least go to a party this year," she whispers to me.

Macy has always wanted to be part of the popular crowds. She had friends and always went to parties, but I never went with her. She's begged me for years to try and fit in with our peers, but I just didn't care. We only had one year left and then

I would more than likely never see them again. My plans were to get out Savannah and travel the world as a teacher. I've already applied to Emory University and a few other schools, but Emory is where I really want to go. Growing up, I was always lonely. As an only child I found myself in the company of nannies and maids, more than my parents. I guess I found friendships with characters in the books I would read and that seemed to suffice any needs I had. Macy would come over and play with me when we were children, and I guess I never understood why she was my friend.

With her long, blonde hair, dazzling blue eyes, and legs for days, she was beautiful and attracted the attention of guys everywhere. I was plain with brown hair, dark eyes, and a small frame that helped me blend in with the crowds. I didn't stick out and I was forever grateful for that.

Sighing, I blew a loose strand of hair out of my face. "Macy, you know that isn't my scene," I replied.

"Nothing is your scene," she jested, rolling her eyes.

I knew that I could exasperate Macy, but she still loved me anyway.

"Then you know that I don't go to parties," I smirked.

"You are so frustrating," she laughed, leaning back in her chair.

I allowed a slight giggle to escape from my lips but then I snapped my mouth shut when I felt a pair of eyes staring right at me.

I hadn't seen the Elite's walk in. But there they were, walking toward the back of the classroom where they always sat. They seemed to make their own assigned seats and the teachers never said a word. I think even the adults were afraid of them.

Ason's deep blue eyes were trained on me, a deep scowl on his face as he stared at me.

Oh, shit.

Why was he looking at me like that?

A few other students noticed that he had stopped and their heads turned to see what had captivated him. Even Macy turned to look at me.

"Ason, why are you stopping? We sit in the back, remember?" Gabby asked, shoving her cousin to keep walking.

Fire red hair flashed past me as Gabby moved around Ason and to her seat. Her green eyes glanced at me for a brief moment when she passed, and I shuddered from being in her vision.

Ason began to move again, swiftly walking down the aisle and as he passed me. I took in the sweet aroma of his cologne and felt the air around me thicken to the point that I almost couldn't breathe. Once he was to his seat, I finally found my breath again. Everyone else shifted in their seats and turned their attention to the front of the room as our teacher, Mrs. Lee, walked into the room.

"What was that?" Macy mouthed to me; her eyes wide with curiosity.

As class began, I couldn't shake the strange feeling of still being watched. I couldn't focus on anything my teacher was saying. All I could think about was Ason and the strange way he had looked at me. We had never spoken before, so there was no reason for him to even know me. But the way he looked at me, that quick glance of disdain, sent a wave of unease flowing through me. Curiosity got the best of me and as I slightly turned my head back, I locked eyes with Ason again.

I quickly turned back around, my cheeks heated and flushed with embarrassment. Ason was glaring daggers my way. I wouldn't have been surprised if he had even growled out at me. In all of the years that we have attended school together, the Elite's had never even spoken to me. Yet alone, looked my way. To them, I was nothing.

So, why was Ason Antoni suddenly looking at me like I had just done something wrong to him?

I really hoped this wasn't a bad omen for how my senior year was going to go.

Chapter 3

Ason

Scarlette had slipped out of class before I had a chance to even gather my things.

Everyone tip-toed around me, not daring to make eye contact with me or Gabby. I knew that Gabby loved the fear that we instilled in everyone around us, but I hated it. Our lives were intertwined with evil and power and those forces oozed out of us like a sore.

Gabby smirked as one of the cheerleaders jumped out of her way. Shaking my head, I grabbed my books and swiftly began moving toward the door. I kept quiet and allowed our classmates to fear me because it was necessary to our lifestyle. Savannah was filled with dangerous mafia families and even though we never openly admitted to it, the entire city knew we were the heirs to the next mafia dynasty. Our kingdom had been built by our fathers and mothers and we would benefit from the blood they had spilled before any of us had been born.

Sure, we had money, but that wasn't what gave us the power and envious looks from those who wanted to be us. It was the danger behind what our lives meant that made us so enticing. Every girl wanted to fuck us and all of the guys wanted to be us. It was like that for our parents and it would be like that for us forever, too.

"Ason, where are you going?" Gabby asked, turning as she noticed that I wasn't walking into our class together.

Shrugging my shoulders, I spoke without looking at her. "Not in the mood for class right now," I snapped.

Gabby rolled her eyes and laughed. "What crawled up your ass?"

She knew she was getting on my nerves, but honestly, Gabby didn't give a shit. We were second cousins, but really, we were more like brother and sister. We were born less than a year apart and had spent every moment of our childhood together. She knew which of my buttons to push, and loved to jab those fuckers until I lit up like a Christmas tree. Her personality and spirit were just as fiery as the red hair she inherited from her mother, Gia, who happened to be my father's cousin.

"Nothing, just don't feel like listening to Mr. Pitman talk," I said, as I walked past her.

"Hey, I know about your punishment," she said, her voice dripping with happiness at my shitty circumstances. "Isn't rule number one that you stop skipping class?" she asked, wagging her eyebrows.

Shrugging, I smirked at her. "Beats me. Besides, I won't skip all day," I yelled back.

I didn't bother to look back or listen to anything she said as I sauntered toward the exit. Teachers saw me leaving, but just like the students here, they were too petrified of me to say anything. My father threw money around this school all of the time to keep me from getting kicked out. They knew the rumors behind the Antoni name and none of them wanted to see if they were true or not.

I pushed open the metal doors and made a bee-line for the student parking lot filled with luxury vehicles that cost as much as most people's homes. My red BMW shined against the early morning sunlight. Pulling a cigarette out of my pocket, I lit the butt and then inhaled the smoke. Leaning against my car, I stared at the two-story brick building of Savannah Royal Academy. Our school earned its name from the various royal history that made their marks in our city. While none of us were truly kings or queens, most of us felt that way from our prestigious status.

I fucking hated it all.

None of this shit really mattered when you thought about it. Sure, money was great to have, but it couldn't fill the emptiness that sat heavy in my heart. No matter how much my parents gave me, I never felt whole. The void that kept me in my constant miserable state continued to grow until one day, I feared that it may completely consume me.

I took another puff of my cigarette before dropping it to the pavement and stomping it with my Italian leather shoes. As much as I wanted to stay out here forever, I knew that I had to get to class eventually. I was on the baseball team—a requirement with our school that each student had to partake in a club or sport—and my coach would have my ass if he found out I skipped a whole day.

Crossing my arms, I leaned my head against the roof of my car and closed my eyes. The warmth from the sunlight felt good on my skin. Images of Scarlette, the quiet girl who always seemed to elude us, sparked in my mind. I knew nothing about her other than the fact that she never was seen at the parties we all attended on the weekends. She seemed to float through the halls like a ghost; she was physically there but no one seemed to notice her.

Well, no one but me.

Ever since middle school, Scarlette had intrigued me. She didn't flaunt her tits in my face or try and become best friends with Gabby. Every girl at our school had fought for a spot with us—the Elite. Sure, I had fucked my way through most of Savannah's private schools, but I had never honestly cared about any of the girls I had been with. They were all too forward, too stuck up, too greedy for me. They wanted the lifestyle I lived and none cared about me as a person because if they had ever cared enough to get to know me on a deeper level, they would have figured out how fucked up I really am.

But with Scarlette, she never seemed interested in any of us and that was what had attracted me to her in the first place. She was a good girl. Beautiful and smart and everything that most guys would kill to have. She would go on one day to be successful and live a happy life. A smile crept over my lips at the thought. She was the type of girl who deserved that type of life. But me, I would remain here in Savannah, moving into my father's career as a made man and be perpetually miserable for the rest of my life.

"Hey, Ason, you going to skip all day?" I heard a voice call out from across the parking lot.

Anger flooded me as I opened my eyes and was taken away from my thoughts of Scarlette. I knew it was ridiculous. Thinking about her was wrong. I was wrong. Plus, I was already breaking one of my father's new rules set for me.

"Fuck off, Talon," I quipped.

Laughter filled the air. Talon was my cousin and best friend. We were close and even had been on my ass to straighten up lately. For Talon, making it into our father's world was his main goal in life. He loved the power we held, while I was ready to give it away at any given moment. I had secretly applied to a few colleges and after seeing Scarlette take an Emory University pamphlet one day from the front office, I applied there, too. It was a long shot, especially when I was expected to take over the Antoni Mafia Family one day, but I had to try. And, I had to try and keep an eye on Scarlette, too. Even if she had no clue that I was watching her.

"So, aren't you on punishment?" he asked, slapping my shoulder. His golden hair seemed to shine against the blazing sunlight. Talon's wide frame shook as he chuckled. He was built like a brick wall which made him the perfect linebacker for our football team. Not only did Talon have the Antoni Family Mafia on his side, but he was a powerhouse in size. The lethal combination made people fear him more. Well, every except for me. To me, Talon was my little cousin who loved to throw partis and act wild. Out of all of us, he was the least of us to worry about.

Damn, did everyone know that I was in trouble? I hated how our parents talked so much.

"Does it matter?" I asked, rolling my eyes. "I'm going to do whatever the fuck I want anyway."

This only caused Talon to laugh more. "I swear, I don't know who I need to worry about more; you or Micah," he whistled.

In reality, I was probably the only one of us truly lost. Micah was wild and reckless and had Hollywood good looks, but he always knew when to stop pushing the boundaries. I guess I was the more silent, crazy one. No one ever really knew what I was going to do—including myself.

"I guess not," he said, kicking the tire of my car. "Seriously though, are you going to do what your dad says?" he asked, all trace of humor gone.

I had to pause before responding. I knew that my parents were fed up with my shitty attitude and were tired of paying to get me out of trouble. Still, I wasn't sure I was ready to face Scarlette. No one knew how I felt about her. She was a secret that I wanted to keep all to myself, because in all honesty, she was too good for a guy like me.

"I guess we will see," I said, shoving off my car and walking back toward the school.

I spent the rest of the day going through the motions of school, while trying not to think about tomorrow afternoon.

CHAPTER 4

SCARLETTE

The alarm on my nightstand rang way too early.

I wasn't ready for the day. I had been up all night with a strange sense of foreboding that I just couldn't pin point. Macy and I had stayed up late on FaceTime as she showed off several outfits, she planned to wear this upcoming weekend. I still wasn't too keen on the idea of going to one of the wild parties thrown by our classmates, but Macy didn't seem to be showing any signs of giving up.

Despite me telling her that I really didn't want to go, she continued to pull clothes that she swore would look fantastic on me. Rolling out of bed, I made my way to my en-suite bathroom and showered before dressing in my purple and gold skirt and blazer uniform. Pulling my hair up in a high ponytail, I raced downstairs where I was welcomed by Angelie, our maid.

"Good morning, Miss Scarlette," she greeted me, as I walking into the kitchen.

My mom was on a business call as she smiled my way. There was a plate filled with scrambled eggs, turkey bacon, and whole wheat toast ready for me on the kitchen island bar. I knew this had been prepared by our chef and not my mom.

I saddled up to the bar and began eating. I watched as my mom paced the kitchen, taking sips of her steaming coffee in between talking to whoever was on the other line. All my life, I had craved for more attention from my mom. Now don't get me wrong; I have a great life. I have parents who provide everything I would ever need, but they are rarely around. Sometimes, I don't mind being alone, but there are times when I wish they would notice me.

Moving the phone away from her ear, mom turned to face me. "Have a good day at school today," she says, flashing a smile.

Just at that moment, dad waltzed into the kitchen, carrying his black leather briefcase and dressed in a sleek, black suit.

"Good morning, Scarlette," he said, reaching for a cup of coffee.

"Hi," I said, through a mouth full of eggs.

"Your mother and I will both be working late tonight, but I have instructed the chef to prepare a dinner for you," he told me, before taking a sip of his coffee.

I admired my parents for their work ethic and motivation to succeed in their respective careers, but part of me still wished for a day when they would want to slow down and spend time with me.

"That's ok. I have tutoring after school today," I explained.

Dad raised his brows at me. "I love your enthusiasm for academics, but you don't need to work, Scarlette."

I knew that my parents couldn't understand why I would subject myself to staying after school, just to tutor someone for little to no pay. However, it was better than having to join a club or sport.

"I don't mind it," I say, shrugging my shoulders. "Besides, it gives me something to do," I say, my tone bleeding with sadness.

My dad shoots me and look and for a brief moment, I see pain radiating from him. Just as he goes to open his mouth, his phone rings, and I know that he has to take the call. I turn my attention back to my food and my dad slips out of the kitchen.

By the time I make it to school, Macy is already waiting for me at my locker. We walk to class together and I spend the rest of the day focusing on not being alone.

When the day is over, I make my way toward the library where our tutoring sessions are held. The expansive space looks more like something you would find on a college campus, rather than a high school.

As I walk inside, I spot Mrs. Miller, the counselor over the tutoring department. She waves me over and I smile as I walk through the rows and rows of books.

"Scarlette, I'm so glad you are here. No one else showed up to tutor today..." she begins frantically.

I see her holding a folder and she seems rather nervous. I've never seen her this frazzled before. Her eyes narrowed and she moved in closer to me, lowering her voice as she began to whisper. "Now, if you don't want to work with this student, I will understand."

Her voice is shaky and confusion settles over me. Why would I not want to work with the assigned student? Mostly, it was athletes and students who were trying to get into Harvard or Yale and needed additional help on work. I had never turned down anyone I had been assigned to, so this was truly flabbergasting to me.

"I don't mind. I mean, how bad can they be?" I asked, chuckling nervously.

Mrs. Miller was making me uncomfortable. Her eyes shifted to the small conference room to the right of us and that was when I realized why Mrs. Miller was acting so strange. Sitting at the head of a table, leaning back in the black leather chair, was Ason Antoni. A deep scowl settled on his face as he noticed my staring. My heart dropped to the pits of my stomach and I suddenly felt ill. A nervous sweat began to form over my forehead and I was sure that my face had paled. Of course, Mrs. Miller was frantic. The savage mafia king was sitting in that room, just waiting for someone to come in and help me.

Hesitating, I sucked in a deep breath as I adjusted my backpack on my shoulder. "Um..." I couldn't seem to form words as I just stood there, frozen in place, and staring back at Ason.

"Are you ok?" Mrs. Miller asked, bringing me out of the fog my mind was stuck in.

Nodding, I croaked out a, "Yes."

"If you need me, I will be in my office," Mrs. Miller explained, before she left me to fend for myself.

As I began to walk toward the room, my legs trembled and I swear, I thought I was going to fall. As I approached the door to the conference room, I felt the air around me shift and a heavy tension threatened to steal my breaths.

"Hi, I'm Scarlette and I am here to tutor you," I said, my voice shaking.

I wasn't sure what had come over me. I had been in school with Ason Antoni since elementary school. I had walked the same halls as him and sat in classrooms with him. But this felt different. I had never been close to him—alone with him and something about this felt way too private and intimate.

Ason continued to stare at me like a predator does its prey. I gulped walking through the threshold of the doorway. I moved to a chair across from him and sat down. His eyes never left me, even when he shifted in his seat.

"I know who you are," he seethed, his voice laced with anger.

Shock spilled through me at that statement. How did Ason Antoni know who I was? Sure, we had gone to school together practically forever, but I never thought he noticed anyone outside of the Elites and those that managed to get a spot in their inner circle.

"Oh," was all I managed to say.

I pulled out the file that Mrs. Miller handed me and opened it. Inside, were lists of assignments that Ason was missing along with worksheets he could complete. I took a moment going through them, pausing and taking my time while I composed myself.

Leaning back, Ason ran a hand through his hair. Sighing, he grabbed the folder from my hands and grunted. I was taken aback by the action and must have looked startled because for a second, he almost looked sorry for snatching the papers from me.

"I can do this, you don't need to stay," he rumbled out.

Grabbing a pen lying on the table, he began to scribble something on the math sheet. He was digging into the paper and I feared he may put a hole right into the wooden table.

"That's great, but I have to stay here with you. If you need any help..." I began, but he rudely cut me off. Shaking his head angrily, Ason's hair fell over his eyes. Swiftly, he shoved the loose hair away from his face and something about that seemingly simple movement made my heart stutter. Ason was incredibly hot and it was almost unfair for him to be this attractive. Even simple gestures were sexy.

"I don't need your help. I just have to sign in to prove I showed up. You can run along now," he stated, waving his hands as though he were shooing away a dog.

Frustrated, I felt a fire ignite inside of me. I realized that there was a hierarchy at this school and I was at the bottom of the list. But that still didn't give him a right to dismiss me and treat me as though I wasn't good enough for him to talk to.

Before I knew what I was doing, I slammed my hand down on the table and a burning sensation filled my palm. "Look, I get that you think you are better than me, but I refuse to be talked down to like this," I yelled.

Clamping my mouth closed, I was shocked by my reaction. Sure, over the years I had grown angry at how people here at this school idolized the Elites, but never had I been brave enough to vocalize such a thing. Especially, in front of Ason Antoni—the king of the Elites.

Ason chuckled, only sending me further into a dark rage. "Don't get your panties twisted," he snarled. "I'm done anyway," he said, shoving the math papers back toward me.

I caught them before they flew off the edge of the table. Ason had, indeed, completed each of the math problems and they were all correct. I even double checked his work and the answers.

"How did you do those so fast? I mean, don't you need help with math?" I asked, completely baffled by this.

Ason went to stand and he straightened out his uniform blazer. "Are we done here?" he asked.

All I could do was nod. As we went to leave, I finally found the courage to speak again. "Wait, we are supposed to be here for an hour," I said, stopping him in the doorway.

Ason turned and those blazing eyes stared back at me, captivating me. "I won't tell if you won't. And... I know how to do the work, I just chose not to," he stated.

"Why would you intentionally fail?" I shout out.

Shrugging, Ason seemed to look away from me, as though just the mere sight of me caused him pain.

"It doesn't really matter," he said softly.

"Well, it does to me. You are smart and have the entire world at your fingertips. Why would you purposely get into trouble? I'm sure you would rather be anywhere else than here right now," I said.

He paused, seeming shocked by my outburst. I doubted if anyone had ever really called Ason out before. Especially, not someone like me. A nobody at this school.

Ason took his final step out of the door, but not before saying, "Maybe I just don't care."

I sat in the empty room in silence, the humming of the air conditioner the only sound. I couldn't believe that I had spoken to an Elite that way, or that I had uncovered something about Ason that I doubted anyone else knew. That last part saddened me, but it also gave me a strange sense of happiness, too. I guess I wasn't the only one who was lonely in a big world.

CHAPTER 5

ASON

The crack of a ball hitting my baseball bat filled my ears. The sun was hot and the air was humid as I ran down to first base. My coach was yelling for me to go faster, but I just didn't have the energy in me to move anymore. Ever since my conversation with Scarlette, I had felt uneasy. There was a strange calmness about her, but a beautiful sadness that I felt like I could relate to. While I had watched her for years, silently observing her movements from afar, I had never seen her really look happy. Sure, at times, she smiled and laughed with her friend, Macy, but other than that, she seemed to want to remain unseen.

To me, it was hard to understand how someone as beautiful as Scarlette could go unnoticed. Nothing about her was plain; from her long, brown locks to her stunning hazel eyes, she was perfection. She didn't wear her shirts too low or her skirts too short. She didn't shameless flirt with the Elite or the other jocks and popular kids at school. She came to school, worked hard, and then went home. I always wondered what she did on the weekends. The rest of us at school partied at each other's houses or on someone's land. Every time I was with a girl, I always wished it was Scarlette.

I had never considered myself a man with a moral compass. What was wrong for most people, wasn't necessarily viewed the same for me. I grew up in a world where killing was the norm and getting what you wanted came at any price. A girl like Scarlette deserved a guy who knew the difference from right and wrong and would provide for her the right way. She deserved flowers and all that stuff that girls fawned over. That just wasn't me. And, it wasn't for lack of seeing those things in my life. My dad constantly worshiped my mother and I knew he loved her and only her, but there was something dark inside of me that kept me from wanting or showing love.

"Ason, pay attention," I heard coach Butler shout angrily.

The fog in my head began to disappear and I realized I was still standing on first base, and a runner was heading right for me. I had completely zoned out.

I began sprinting to second base, with Tyler, one of my teammates, closely on my heels. Dirt and sand from the infield picked up as I stepped on second base, and then slid into third. As I stood and dusted the dirt off my baseball pants, I sighed as coach jogged toward me. I was about to get an ass chewing.

"What was that, Antoni?" he shouted my way.

I could tell he was holding back the real rage he wanted to unleash on me. No one dared to really go off on me. They knew all too well what would happen if I told my father. Even if I deserved it, people could just disappear if I wanted them to.

"Sorry, I got distracted," I mumbled.

A few girls who stood in the bleachers waved over as both coach Butler and I looked their way. Coach Butler shook his head, but then his face softened.

"Listen, I get it. You are a good-looking kid and it's fun to chase the girls. Still, you need to get your head into the game. Those girls will only mess you up. Get what I'm saying, Ason?" he asks, slapping my shoulder.

"Sure," I grumbled out.

I swiped at a bead of sweat on my forehead and made sure to focus the rest of practice. Coach thought I had been distracted by the girls in the bleachers, but really, the only girl worth gaining my attention wouldn't be caught dead flirting with me at practice.

After practice, I showered in our locker room and then made my way to the parking lot. Scarlette was walking across the pavement, her head down, as she moved toward an Audi SUV. She was so fucking beautiful that it almost hurt to look at her. I hated the sadness that radiated from her eyes. It made me wonder if anyone ever tried to erase that tragic look from her. Suddenly, Scarlette glanced up. Surely, she felt my stare and as her gaze moved to mine, she tensed and stopped walking.

We stood there, across the parking lot, staring at one another like strangers. Only a few hours earlier, we had been in a heated conversation as I walked out of our tutoring session early. I knew that I had pissed her off and for some strange reason, that had weighed heavily on me. Typically, I didn't care if I pissed off girls. It was sort of the norm for me, but there was something inside of me that didn't want to hurt her.

Shaking her head, Scarlette looked away, breaking our contact, and continued walking to her vehicle. Anger floored me and I thought about rushing over to her and asking her why she always looked so lonely, but I thought better of it. Why should I care?

I got to my car, threw my baseball bag into the backseat, and then sped out of the parking lot as my tires squealed and smoked. Racing through the streets of Savannah, I blasted my music as I tried to drown out all thoughts of Scarlette. Only, I wished it were that easy.

My phone ringing over the cars speakers brought me out of my funk.

"Hello," I clipped.

"Hey, I'm finishing up at the gym and was going to head over to watch Micah race," Talon said.

I could hear the sounds of the gym in the background and he sounded out of breath as he spoke. The last thing I wanted to do was to watch Micah tear through the alleys of Savannah in one of his dangerous and illegal races. Why he thought it was fun to drag race for money, was beyond me.

"I'm not sure," I sighed. "I really just want to head home," I told him.

"Why don't you head over here with me?" Talon pushed.

"Ask Gabby. She could use some muscle," I stated through the phone.

I heard Talon chuckle at that. I used to pick on Gabby when we were little because she was always so thin. She had filled out and added curves to her figure as a teenager, but she could benefit from some gym time.

"Nah man, Gabby is shopping or some shit like that," he laughed. "Why are you trying to back out of this?" he asked, obviously frustrated with me.

I knew he was upset that I had been absent lately, but I just needed some alone time to get my thoughts together. Scarlette was really messing with my head.

"I will think about it," I stated, though we both knew that meant that I wasn't going to show up.

My normal activities just didn't feel fun and exciting any-more. And, I wasn't sure if anything ever would again.

Chapter 6

Scarlette

Walking into the empty house, the darkness almost seemed comforting.

Moving through the large foyer, my footsteps echoed all around me. I turned on lights in the hallway and then the kitchen. The pristine, all white kitchen with state-of-the-art appliances shined as I walked into the room. There was a note from the chef, with instructions on how to heat up the dinner he had prepared and placed in the refrigerator.

After reheating my chicken alfredo, I sat alone at the kitchen island. The conversation—if you could even call it that—with Ason still weighed heavily on me. He didn't even care enough to stick around for his required tutoring session. After he had left, I had stayed in the room and read through his files. His grades were garbage and he had been assigned tutoring so that he could gain his credits to graduate. Ason didn't come off to me as the type of guy who cared about anything like grades, but still, I was sure that he would want to graduate. I was sure that Ason hated me and only because I wasn't an Elite.

Taking a bite of my alfredo, I savored the creamy sauce and the hint of garlic. Sighing, I grabbed my phone and began scrolling through my social media accounts. To be honest, I wasn't sure why I had let Macy talk me into even having social media. I rarely posted anything and only a handful of people liked or followed my posts anyway. I was a nobody at this school.

My phone chimed and I jumped at the sudden sound. A text from Macy lit up the screen.

Macy: Party tomorrow night!

Ugh, I hated that she wasn't letting this up. First, showing me outfits, she was picking out the other night and now confirming it.

Me: I may be sick.

Macy: No chance. I will pick you up at 8 tomorrow!

I dropped my phone down onto the white, marble counter and scarfed down the rest of my dinner. I had no idea what time my parents would be home and I have an English essay to write. I placed my empty plate in the dishwasher and then went upstairs to my bedroom. Walking into my room, I padded across the soft carpet on my way to my ensuite bathroom. My room was painted a soft lavender and my bedspread, curtains, and wall décor all had a wildflower to feel. I detested the colors. I wish more than anything that I could just paint my walls red or blue or some wild color, but my mom would never allow such a thing in our house. She had hired a designer and every few years, she redecorated to match whatever aesthetically pleasing theme was in style.

After showering in my tile shower, I fell into bed with my laptop and began working on my essay. Once my eyes grew too heavy to focus any longer, I feel asleep and didn't wake again until morning.

Walking into school, I could feel the buzz around the halls.

Everyone was talking about the party tonight and it sounded like most of the school planned on being there. I had never paid much attention to talk about who was throwing a party and where, but since Macy was basically forcing me to go against my will, I took the liberty of listening as I went to my locker and began gathering my books for the day.

"Hey, which outfit did you like?" Macy asked, leaning against my locker.

I pulled out my laptop and Calculus textbook and turned to face her. "What?"

"I sent you like three pictures of outfits I had decided would look good," she said, sighing as I stared back at her.

"Oh, sorry. I fell asleep last night. I'll look at them later," I explained.

Macy pushed herself off my locker. "Can you at least pretend to be excited? I mean, do you know how many people would kill to go to parties like the one we are going to?"

I knew she had a point, but I still didn't really care. Parties just weren't my thing.

"I promise, I will make an effort to smile," I said sarcastically.

Macy laughed and looped her arm through mine. We walked into class and I spent the rest of the day trying not to think about the party.

Macy placed a layer of pink lip gloss over my lips as she smiled down at me.

I stared at my reflection in the mirror and hardly recognized myself. My long, brown hair was swept up in a high ponytail and my hazel eyes were lined with thick, black eyeliner. Flecks of gold reflected over my eyelids and my plunging neckline had me constantly pulling my shirt up, only to reveal more of my stomach than I liked.

"Will you stop fidgeting," Macy scolded, as she placed the lid back over the lip gloss.

"This shirt is a little too much," I stated, still staring at myself.

"Whatever. You look hot," Macy smirked.

I stood from the chair in front of my vanity and tried to pull down the jean skirt that barely covered my ass. Macy had lost her mind!

"I can't leave my house looking like this. I look like a hooker!" I practically yelled out.

Macy only laughed as she added more mascara to her own eyes. She leaned over the vanity and glanced at me from the mirror. "Well, maybe you will get some action," she said, winking.

Macy didn't mind showing off a little skin—well, a lot of skin. Her long legs were wearing tight, black leather pants and her gold sequin tube top showed off her ample breasts. She looked amazing and I felt silly standing next to her.

"I don't want any action," I mumbled.

"Well, maybe it might help you relax," she laughed, grabbing my hand and leading me toward the bedroom door.

We arrived at the party in less than ten minutes.

The street was lined with cars and part of me wondered how any of the neighbors hadn't called the cops due to excessive noise. Though, part of me believed these kids parents were probably rarely home, just like mine weren't.

"Whose house is this?" I asked, as Macy parked her white Range Rover in front of a dark house.

"Mark Landis, the quarterback for the football team," she said.

Mark Landis was your typical jock. His parents were international attorneys and never home. Even though I wasn't in his inner circle of friends, even I knew that Mark Landis threw large parties weekly. He was practically an orphan since he was without his parents more than he was with them.

We got out of the car and the thumping of the music had my body shaking. Walking up to the brightly lit mansion, I gulped down my nervousness. It was strange how awkward I felt, while people smiled and laughed as they talked on the front lawn. This was normal for them.

Comfortable.

I followed Macy into the house and the air was electric. Music seemed to fill every space of the house and red solo cups littered the ground as we walked through the grand foyer and toward a formal living room. A few girls in short skirts were dancing on a white couch, no doubt, destroying the fabric. However, I doubted anyone would notice. These people had enough money to purchase new couches in the morning if they so desired. Plus, I was sure Mark Landis would hire a cleaning crew to come in and erase any damage done from this party. That was just how our perfect, twisted little world worked.

"Macy!" a few girls squealed, as they waved her toward the kitchen.

Macy waved back and began dancing and swaying to the beat of the rap music as she headed toward the group. I had no choice but to follow her. There was no way in hell I was going to get lost in this sea of douchebags that I called classmates.

As I pushed back a couple making out in the hallway, I felt a strange sensation wash over me. I felt like I was being watched, which was beyond insane because half the people in here were so drunk, they could barely see straight. A drunk guy I recognized from my chemistry class stumbled past me, grabbing onto me for support.

"Sorry," he mumbled, the word barely recognizable through his drunken haze.

Swatting his hand off my shoulder, I glanced around as the eerie feeling continued to creep over me. "It's ok," I stated, watching him hold onto the wall for support as he kept walking.

Spinning, I finally found a pair of eyes locked on me. Narrowing my gaze, I stared back through the crowd at the one person who I had hoped more than anything I wouldn't see tonight.

Ason.

Damn, I knew I shouldn't have come to this party.

As our gazes locked, Ason's jaw ticked. Anger flooded through me as I suddenly noticed a black-haired beauty on his lap. She was nibbling on his ear and giggling, while his hand rested on her waist. They sat in the corner of one of the large sofas in what appeared to be a family den. The brown leather sofa was large enough for at least seven people, yet this girl felt it necessary to sit right on top of Ason.

Shaking my head, I turned my eyes away from them and stormed into the kitchen where Macy was standing among her other friends. As I approached, one of the girls Sara Beth, handed me a red solo cup filled with a pink liquid.

Macy instantly shook her head. "No, Scarlette doesn't drink," she stated, reaching for the cup in front of me.

Jerking the cup away from her, I placed the cup to my lips and downed the sweet liquid. It was good, but had a strong kick at the end. At that moment, I didn't care what was inside of the cup.

Macy's eyes shot daggers my way and the girls cheered as I slammed the empty cup onto the granite countertop.

"Wow, Scarlette. I had no idea you knew how to party," Sara Beth said.

Macy leaned in and whispered in my ear. "You don't have to drink, Scarlette. That punch is spiked with vodka."

She appeared nervous and I didn't want to her to blame herself. Macy had begged me for years to go to these parties with her. What I was doing right now wasn't because of her. Honestly, I had no real idea why I decided to let all of my inhibitions go and try to drown out the anger ringing in my head right now. Or maybe, it was the alcohol.

"I guess it's time that I enjoy myself for once," I said, anger lacing my words.

Macy looked at me like I had grown two heads. Confusion filled her features, but she didn't try to stop me.

Sara Beth handed me another cup and I drank more. "Slow down, that will get you messed up fast," she warned.

Right now, I didn't care about warnings. I wanted the ache in my chest to go away. I wanted to become numb. To no think about Ason and the skank sitting in his lap. I hated how terrible I felt and none of it made any sense. Ason wasn't someone who I had ever cared about before. He was an Elite, someone out of my reach. He was bad. Untouchable.

Still, though, I couldn't help but think about those danger-ous, brooding eyes with every sip I took.

CHAPTER 7

ASON

Sometimes, I prefer noise to the silence.

With silence, you can hear your own thoughts.

Your raging heart beats pound so loudly in your ears, that it's almost painful.

But with noise, you can drown out everything bad in the world. All of those pesky voices in your head seem to just fade away and you only worry about the voices on the outside.

Right now, I was grateful more than ever for the loud rap music blaring from the speaker behind me. As Cameron, a cheerleader from school, whispered in my ear, I could barely make out the scandalous words she was spewing. She wiggled on my lap, causing my dick to stir underneath her. Her hands were freely groping me and I knew that within the hour, I would have her upstairs and on her back. She would be screaming out my name as I pounded into her pussy, and then I would ignore her Monday morning at school.

I didn't do relationships, but it didn't stop half the females at school and in Savannah, from trying to tie me down. Each girl thought that they could tame me. Make me reconsider my decision to not date.

Talon walked past the couch, a blonde who I didn't recognize on his arm, as he headed toward the large, spiral staircase in the foyer. Chuckling, I laughed to myself as he winked my way. Talon at times, could be worse than me. However, he had a tendency to get caught up in each girl and would date them for a few weeks before he became bored and found himself on to the next girl. His escapades exhausted me.

As I watched Talon head up the stairs, something caught my eye and I felt my heart skip a beat.

The last girl I would have ever expected to see at this party—any party actually—walked through the front door.

I recognized her friend, Macy, first. Though, Macy attended these parties frequently, I had never seen Scarlette accompany her. A flash of rage tore through me as a timid looking Scarlette followed closely behind her friend. She was nervous. Petrified. But worse, she didn't really look like the Scarlette I was used to seeing. Her outfit was revealing and way too extreme for someone as beautiful as she was. Scarlette had a natural beauty that the girls at this party would kill for her. She didn't need to show off those delicious curves or ample breasts to get attention. Just her presence alone was enough. Something about seeing Scarlette dressed like she was sent a fire though my body. I didn't want her to look like the other girls.

"What are you staring at?" Micah asked, as he strolled into the room.

"Nothing," I gritted out.

I heard Micah chuckle as he walked past me and over to the girls who were eyeing him. My eyes betrayed me as they continued to stare at Scarlette. Suddenly, Scarlette began looking around the room, like she could feel my eyes boring into her. Even though I should have looked away—I needed to look away—I just couldn't.

When Scarlette's eyes found mine, there was a spark in the air and an energy that pushed between us. In my mind, I pleaded with her to look away. She shouldn't look at me like...she wanted me. Like I was someone worthy of her.

I wasn't.

The way Scarlette looked at me was primal and I hated that I felt a strong desire for her. As quickly though as our spark ignites, it died down as she huffed and stormed away. Part of me was glad that she had left in an angry storm. Still, another part of me wanted to know where she was going. I had to know why she was here tonight.

Cameron's tongue slipped along my jaw and I felt sick to my stomach. Earlier tonight, I had planned on fucking Cameron, but right now, I wanted to get her as far away from me as possible. Shoving her, Cameron fell off my lap and landed on the hardwood floor below.

"What was that for?" she asked, red flaming her cheeks from embarrassment.

I didn't bother giving her a response, instead, I stepped over her and headed down the hall. I was a glutton for punishment; I knew that for sure. Seeking out Scarlette was only going to end in pain for me, but I just couldn't worry about that. Honesty, I welcomed the hurt I would surely feel by the end of the night. At least, I wouldn't be numb.

I had no idea where to start in looking for Scarlette. I shoved past people dancing and drinking and walked toward the living room. Mark Landis wasn't really a friend, but I had been to enough of his parties to know my way around his house. Opening the glass French doors leading to the pool and patio area. Two topless girls walked past me, winking as they headed toward the pool. Music played outside, too, and a couple of guys were smoking a joint as they sat in the steaming hot tub.

My eyes roamed the backyard and I felt a sense of re-lief when I didn't see Scarlette anywhere outside. Turning, I moved back inside and opened a bedroom door that led to the master bedroom. A couple was busy getting it on and yelled, as I opened and then quickly closed the door back. Frustration consumed me each time I walked into a room or darkened hallway and didn't find Scarlette. Finally, I made my way to the kitchen where a group of girls were huddled around the large, glass punch bowl on the kitchen island. Standing in the center of the girls was Scarlette. A glazed over expression covered her face.

Leaning against the doorframe, I crossed my arms as I watched her. I felt like I could finally relax a little. I knew I had no business stalking Scarlette like this. Still, I knew I had to keep an eye on her. She was too good, too naïve, too sweet to be at a party like this. Drugs, drinking, and wild sex should not be Scarlette's scene.

Laughing, Scarlette spotted me and held up the red solo cup in her hand, smiling, before downing the cup. She swayed a bit as she placed the now empty cup on the counter. She was definitely drunk and that didn't sit right with me. I wondered if she had ever been drunk before. My eyes found Macy and she looked nervous, watching Scarlette let loose. That didn't sit right with me either.

My phone buzzed in my pocket and as I pulled the device out, I spotted Gabby's name on the screen.

Gabby: Hey, where are you?

Me: At a party.

Gabby: No shit. I'm here, too. Where are you?

My head began to pound. Gabby wasn't supposed to be here. I didn't like for her to parties when the rest of us; myself, Talon, and Micah, were drinking or getting high. Even though Gabby is an Elite and most guys are terrified of her, none of us liked the idea of her at a place where we would have to keep an eye on her. Trouble seems to follow Gabby everywhere she goes, and I wasn't in the mood to babysit her right now.

Me: I'm in the kitchen. Where are you?

Gabby: Outside, I just pulled up.

Me: Stay in your car.

I quickly typed out a text to Talon and told him to go outside and make sure Gabby left. I wasn't about to leave the kitchen where Scarlette was. Placing my phone back in my pocket, I looked up again and a new found rage settled inside of me.

Troy Allen was standing next to Scarlette, smiling down at her as his hand swept over her bare arm. Macy and the other girls were now dancing by the kitchen table and had no idea what Scarlette was doing. Troy leaned down and whispered something in Scarlette's ear, causing a deep crimson blush to heat her cheeks. Any control I had left in that moment. I knew Troy Allen well. He had a way of sweet-talking girls into his bed and most ended up not remembering anything the next morning. He sought after girls who were drunk or high—making him one of the lowest assholes you could find. I didn't mess with guys like that.

Approaching them, Troy's gazed fixed on mine and I saw the defeat in his eyes. He knew better than to mess with me. Everyone knew what my father was capable of, and no one dared to find out if I was just like him, too.

Taking a step back, he let his hand drop to his side and Scarlette flashed him a confused look. Her glazed over eyes followed his until they reached me. Her smile faded and a storm flashed across her features. Clouds raged in her eyes and for some reason, that made me smile.

"Uh, Hey, Ason," Troy said, taking another step away from me. His back bumped into the stove and I saw him wince from pain.

"Get the hell out of here, Troy," I growled out.

Troy nodded, before retreating for the living room. He knew better than to dare and open his mouth to argue with me. I stared down at Scarlette as her hate-filled eyes bore into me.

"What are you doing?" she slurred, swatting at my arm.

When her fingers touched my skin, I felt a spark of energy course through me. I knew she felt it, too, because even through her drunken haze, I heard her gasp and she quickly pulled back from me.

"You need to go home," I tell her, through clenched teeth.

Hands on her hips, Scarlette attempts to stand up straight, but her legs almost give out and she has to reach for the counter to steady herself. "You can't tell me what to do," she slurs again.

At our exchange, Macy approaches. While I can smell the fruity alcohol on her breath, she isn't drunk like Scarlette is. I turn to her and glare and Macy shakes under my stare.

"Hi, I can get her out of here," Macy says nervously.

Shaking my head, I pinch the bridge of my nose as I try to control the anger that is trying to bubble to the surface. "Shouldn't you have been watching your friend?" I ask her.

Macy opens her mouth, but quickly clamps it shut.

"You don't know me," Scarlette cries out, causing both Macy and I to look at her again.

"Do you know who she is?" Macy asks.

I know that Macy must be confused as to why I am even talking to them. I never talk to anyone except f the girls I am about to bang.

"Scarlette is my tutor. I've never seen her here before," I state fiercely.

I have no idea why I even need to explain myself. Macy should be the one answering the questions. She let her friend get drunk on her watch. As I was arguing with Macy, Scarlette had slipped out of my watch again.

Turning, I throw my hands up in the air as I spot Scarlette swaying her hips to the beat of the music while Troy stupidly saddles up next to her. This guy must have a death wish.

Storming out of the kitchen, I stop next to Scarlette as Troy's hand slips to her waist. Before I know what I am doing, I rear my fist back and punch Troy in the face. I hear the deafening crack of bone as blood gushes out of his nose.

"What the hell, man?" Troy cries out, grabbing his nose and falling back.

Scarlette's wide eyes look horrified as she takes in the scene before her.

"Why did you do that?" she asks, but her face looks distraught and her lips are trembling.

Macy, once again, runs up to us and she looks almost as horrified as her friend. My head is spinning and I can't seem to control the rage that now consumes me. My anger intensifies as I take in Macy. If she had only paid better attention to her friend...

"How could you let her drink?" I roar out.

"Me?" Macy questions, as tears begin to form in her eyes.

A group of onlookers pause and watch as our drama-filled scene unfolds. A few look like they want to intervene, but none are that stupid. They would be sealing their own death if they approached me now. "I feel sick," Scarlette suddenly says, hugging her tiny waist. "No, my head hurts," she adds.

Huffing, I exhale a deep breath and then lean down, grabbing Scarlette and hoisting her over my shoulders. She lets out a squeal as she hangs over my shoulder. I begin heading toward the front door, shoving people out of my way and knocking over those who aren't lucky enough to move before I get to them.

Scarlette pounds her tiny fists against my back, but I barely feel her hitting me. Macy follows along behind us, but I don't bother listening to what she is yelling at us. Once I reach the front door, I am welcomed by the cool night air. Moving to the front lawn, I pass a group of students smoking and drinking. None say anything as I storm past them toward my car. Once I reach the sidewalk, I pull my keys out of my pocket and unlock the doors to my vehicle. I place Scarlette down onto the sidewalk and she sways, causing me to hold her up as I fumble with the keys.

"Where are you going with her? She needs to get home," Macy shrieks.

I'm sure she is thinking the worst as I am basically kidnapping her best friend. Though, the irony of the situation isn't lost on me. I may be the most dangerous person in this house, but yet, I'm the one trying to save Scarlette. Being drunk and innocent puts her at risk. Every guy at this party would love to be the one to deflower the sweet girl and then brag about it at school next week. The music still thumped and people were still partying while I struggled to get Scarlette into my car.

Facing Macy, I threw open my back passenger door and began to push Scarlette inside. Her tiny frame tried to put up a fight, but it was no use. She was too far gone to fight back right now.

"I'm taking her home. She isn't safe here and you should know that," I spat out.

Macy looked insulted as she stared back at me. "She's my best friend, of course, she is safe with me," she cried out. "Besides, you don't know where she lives," she yelled.

Scarlette fell across my seats and mumbled something as I slammed the door closed. Macy stood on the sidewalk, the glow of the moonlight illuminating off her angry and terrified face.

Opening the driver's side door, I went to sit down, but not before saying one last thing to Macy. "Don't worry about anything. I have my ways of knowing things," I grunted, before shutting the door in her stunned face. Tearing away from the curb, my tires squealed as my own music began to pump through the speakers. Speeding through Savannah, I kept glancing in my rearview mirror. Scarlette's form lay sprawled across my backseat. I knew that I would have to explain to Scarlette when she sobered up how I knew her address, but I would have to worry about that later. Right now, I needed to get her home and in bed before she puked all over my leather seats.

CHAPTER 8

SCARLETTE

A pounding in my head jolted me from a deep sleep. Like a hammer beating against my skull, I felt like my head would burst at any second. Groaning, I rolled over and a wave of nausea swept over me. Oh no, I was going to be sick. Struggling to sit up, I knew that I needed to get to the bathroom and fast.

As I went to move, my head began to spin as though the world around me was a tilt-a-whirl.

"I wouldn't do that if I were you," a gruff voice said, surprising me.

Rubbing my eyes, I was astounded to see Ason sitting in my white chair beside my window. He was smoking and dropping his ashes onto the white carpet below him. Glancing at the clock on my bedside table, I saw that it was almost five in the morning. Why was Ason at my house?

In my room?

Talking to me?

Suddenly, like a flash of lightning striking down on me, images of last night played through my head like a bad movie.

Drinking punch.

Dancing.

Fighting with Ason.

Oh no, what have I done?

A paralyzing fear washed over me and I crawled back in bed, pulling my sheets over my body. Ason wasn't supposed to be here. In fact, I was pretty sure that he hated me. His scowling face was locked in my mind and it was something I was sure I would never forget.

"What are you doing here?" I ask, my voice dry and scratchy.

My stomach still churned and I felt like I was going to vomit any second now. This couldn't be how I died.

Ason leans forward, placing his hands on his knees as he stares at me. The soft glow from the lights outside filter in through the window and cast a dreamy glow across his features. No one should look as good as Ason does. Honestly, it should be a crime.

A low chuckle erupts from him and I almost tremble under the sound. "Well, after you got drunk last night and almost made a huge mistake, I brought you home." His words came out angry and rough; just like him.

Dancing and drinking several cups of the punch rush my mind and I cringe at the memory. I know that I should probably be thanking him for getting me home safely, but there is something in his tone and mood that makes me feel like he is angry that he had to bring me home at all. I may not remember much from last night, but I am pretty certain that I would never ask Ason—or any of the Elites in general—for a ride home. Especially, when I had gone to the party with Macy. Wait! Macy!

"What happened to Macy? She had driven me to the party," I cried.

Ason only stared at me again. "Your mind must be a jumbled mess. You keep asking questions," he half laughed.

Again, it seemed as though he were insulting me, instead of helping me. "Well, I just don't understand any of this," I began. "I mean, I only talked to you for the first time ever last week. Now, you are sitting in my bedroom after a night I barely remember," I let the words spill out of me. My head still ached and I couldn't fight off the nausea much longer. My mouth opened as a gag erupted.

Ason rushed to the side of the bed, lifting my small trashcan up to me as I hurled over and began vomiting all of the pink liquid from last night. Once I felt like my stomach was empty, I fell back against my pillows. This was just great. Not only had I gotten drunk in front of Ason last night, now I had just puked in front of him. I was sure the entire school would know about this by Monday.

"Thank you," I whispered, as I wiped my mouth with the back of my hand.

Ason scowled as he tied the plastic bag inside of the trash-can.

"Have you ever done this before? Been drunk?" he asked, his narrow eyes seeming to judge me. There was pity there, too, and I wasn't sure which one infuriated me more.

As I shook my head, I instantly regretted the movement. Pain sliced through me and I swear, I felt like my head was going to crack open from the pounding.

"No, never."

Sighing, Ason ran a hand through his dark hair. "I think Macy tried to stop you, but then you were out of control. I grabbed you once a few guys were going to make a move. You know, you have no business being at a party like that," he stated fiercely.

Ason really had a lot of nerve. How much humiliation could I take from him. Even though I felt like death, I forced myself to sit up and look him in the eyes. I caught a glimpse of myself in my dresser mirror and I wanted to scream. My unruly hair was all over the place and my eyes were bloodshot. I'm sure I didn't smell great either.

"Listen, maybe you think you did a good deed last night by bringing the nerdy drunk girl home, but I can take care of myself. Besides, you have no business telling me what I can and can't do. Most of the kids at school believe you are a God or some form of royalty just because..." my words trailed off as I suddenly realized what I was about to say.

Ason's eyes flared red with rage. "Just because what?" he asked, daring me to finish my sentence.

"Just because you think you are powerful," I corrected, though we both knew that wasn't what I had intended to say at all. "You believe the whole world wants to bow down to you."

No, I wanted to tell him that just because he came from mafia royalty, didn't mean that I was one of his peasants. I wasn't one of the girls who fawned over him, hoping to get a glimpse into his dangerous world. I had higher standards for myself.

Ason nodded and his eyes flashed with hurt. It almost caught me off guard. I felt like I may be sick again and I wasn't sure if it was from the hangover I was now experiencing or the thought of insulting and hurting Ason.

Ason stood, his tall frame towering over me as I shrunk against my bedframe. He moved to the edge of the bed, leaning over so that his face was close to mine. "Let me tell you something, you have no idea just how powerful I truly am. If I wanted to hurt you last night or even right now," he said, a faint of a smile creeping over his angered face, "you would be long gone by now. A nice, thank you, would have sufficed," he finished, shooting daggers at me with his heated glare.

I gulped as I stared back at him. We both knew that Ason could destroy my life in one second if he wanted to. But, he hadn't. Instead, he had brought me home. Put me in my bed. Watched me all night...but why?

I knew I should have kept my mouth shut, but the stubborn side of me was out-winning the logical and rational side. "Why did you help me?" I asked.

Something flashed across his face that I couldn't comprehend. It was sudden and fierce and yet, I didn't understand it at all.

Releasing what could only be described as a growl, Ason pushed himself away from my bed and began moving toward my bedroom door. As he opened the door, he turned one last time and looked at me.

"You should be more careful who you let into your house," he warned, and then slammed my door closed.

I winced at the loud bang and my head instantly began hurting again. Tears formed in my eyes and I couldn't hold them back. My body was in pain and my heart was aching. I had no idea what had just happened, but I knew that I would never be the same again.

My phone buzzed on the bedside table and I could barely make out the texts from my parents. Tears blurred my vision, but I was still able to read their apologizes for coming home late last night and leaving early this morning. They hadn't even realized that I had come home drunk. Or, that Ason Antoni—the son of a killer and mafia boss—had spent the night in my bedroom.

Ason's warning or advice-- not sure which it was truly intended to be, rang through my mind. Little did he know that in my world, I was always alone so worrying about who came into my home wasn't on my radar.

My phone buzzed again and this time, I couldn't ignore the sound. Sighing, I grabbed the phone and expected to see another one of the rapid texts, but what I saw shocked the hell out of me.

Ason: Take the Tylenol I left on your dresser. There is a bottle of water, too.

I had to read the text three more times before I actually believed the words were real and not a figment of my imagination. Staring blankly at my phone, so many emotions and questions swirled in my head. How did Ason get my number? Why would he even text me? He was a perplexing creature that I doubted I would ever understand.

Me: Thanks. How did you get my number?

I watched as the tiny bubbles danced across my screen. I knew that I should probably block his number or turn my phone off completely. But instead, I gave in to my own intrigue and waited for his response.

Ason: I added my number to your phone, and yours to mine while you were passed out. You know, you need to be more careful who you trust.

His words of advice were much more like a warning. I didn't trust Ason, that much I knew for sure.

Me: Don't worry, I have never trusted anyone before, so I won't start now.

Ason never wrote back and even though I felt a tiny pang of hurt at this lack of a response, I knew that it was for the best.

CHAPTER 9

ASON

A yawn escaped my mouth as I sat in the white chair, smoking yet another cigarette.

Scarlette lay sprawled out in her bed, her hair in disarray as she lightly snored. I knew when I threw her into my backseat, that I was making a terrible decision.

In fact, Talon and Micah had been calling me all night reminding what a shitty thing I was doing. Scarlette wasn't my problem. I had no business taking her anywhere, but still, I couldn't help but feel a protective urge come over me when I felt like she was in danger. A girl like Scarlette didn't deserve to be hit on my assholes like Troy. The Elites had made a deal with Troy our freshman year. He wanted to throw outrageous and wild parties, but no one really liked Troy. He was cocky, arrogant, and entitled. I guess those adjectives could describe me, too, but I had the mafia behind my name and that was enough to put me into an entirely different universe from the Troy's of the world. Anyway, he had come to me and asked for a business proposition. It was honestly one of the first times in my life that I had felt right making a deal like this. He would pay me to show up at his parties. It started out small. I would show up, take a few selfies with Troy or girls and then people would begin flocking to his house just to get a glimpse of me. Then, when Talon, Micah, and Gabby got into high school, they would come, too, earning themselves a cut of the profit.

All we did was show up and get paid. That and only that was why I was at Troy's party in the first place.

I couldn't stand the people I went to school with and I sure as hell wouldn't voluntarily hang out with them without getting paid. That sort of thinking was ingrained in me. It made me part of the mafia through-and-through.

Still, as I sat in the chair, watching Scarlette, I couldn't help but grow angry at the thought that no one had come to her rescue besides me. Macy was drunk herself and I hadn't heard any parents come home at all. Was Scarlette always alone? Did she have someone to protect her?

I knew it wasn't right for me worry about Scarlette. I knew that inviting her into my world would only put her in danger, but I couldn't help myself from thinking about her. Wanting to be the protector she needed.

When Scarlette finally woke up, her reaction to me being in her bedroom, hadn't been what I had expected. At first, I thought she would thank me. I had sat by her side to make sure she didn't get sick in the middle of the night and choke and die. I had watched her breathing, ensuring she was safe and sound all night. Instead, she was frazzled and almost angered by my presence. From what I had observed of Scarlette over the years, I had only witnessed the timid, shy, and tragically beautiful girl being quiet and reserved. However, I had seen a different side of her that made my dick twinge awake. She had been wild and reckless with her words. She didn't fear or idolize me like every other girl and that made me want her even more.

Even walking out of her room had been one of the hardest things I had ever done. What I had really wanted to do was shut her up with a long kiss that would make her rethink everything she ever thought she knew about the world. I wanted to pull her against my body and let her know that someone—even a dangerous guy like me- cared for her.

I didn't do any of those things though. No, I walked right out the damn door and went straight home. I hadn't made it very

far when I remembered the Tylenol I had found in her med-
icine cabinet. I had gone searching through her house while
she was snoring and in a heavy, drunken sleep. Her house felt
more like a museum than it did a home. The all-white interior
was clean and void of any personal touches. But her room
was another story. It felt like her. Smelled like her. After I had
come back in her room, I had spotted her phone and added
my number, then adding her contact to mine. It was a bold
move, but I needed to know that she would be ok.

On Monday, I almost dreaded going to school.

I had baseball practice and my coach was still pissed at me
for my crappy grades. And, I had a tutoring session with Scarlette. I had called my counselor to see if she could reschedule
me with someone else, but of course, no one would take me
on.

Scarlette had avoided me all day and I was grateful for
it. I wasn't sure how I would have reacted if we had come
face-to-face. Even in the class we had shared, she had shown
up late and sat in the front of the room. When the dismissal
bell rang, she bolted out of the room before I could even
blink.

"Hey, what was wrong with you yesterday?" Talon asked, as
he found me in the halls.

Every Sunday, the Antoni Mafia Family gets together for a family dinner. Typically, it's filled with amazing food, lots of laughter, and at times, fighting. The made men discuss money and their dealings while the rest of us hang out. However, yesterday, I wasn't in the mood to hang out with everyone. I didn't talk to anyone during dinner, and then locked myself in my bedroom the rest of the night.

"Nothing, I just didn't feel like hanging out with you, assholes," I said, watching as Talon glared at me.

"Whatever, man. Gabby said you've been acting weird in class, too," he stated, eyeing me suspiciously. "Then, you left the party early and no one knew where you went."

I knew that he was searching for answers, but I wasn't about to give him any information. Even though we were family, I had to protect the last bit of privacy that I had left. In the mafia, your business is everyone else's. While I still had my own life, I wanted to protect that.

"So what? I had other plans," I said, shrugging my shoulders.

As we walked down the hall, I kept an eye out for Scarlette. She had ghosted me, but later today, she would have to face me when we had our tutoring session.

"Since when do you have plans that don't involve us?"

Talon seemed genuinely insulted that I would have a life outside of my family.

"Why are you asking so many questions?" I asked, stopping by my last class of the day.

"I just think you are hiding something," he responded, a cocky smirk growing.

Talon eyed me carefully. He knew I was full of shit right now, but he also knew that as the oldest of our group, I wasn't the one to mess with.

Stepping closer to Talon, I clenched my fists to my side and kept my eyes locked on him. Talon flinched but never backed down. He may be physically bigger than me, but I am the one to watch out for. Lowering my voice, I made sure that he heard me very clearly.

"Listen to me very carefully. What I do on my own time is my fucking business. If I want to hide something, I'll do it. Watch how you talk to me. I may just be the head of the Antoni Mafia family one day. You wouldn't want to mess with the capo now, would you?" I asked, a sinister smile growing on my face.

Talon's eyes grew wide and I saw a flash of fear strike him briefly. I had never had to step up to one of my family before, but I was tired of the questions and accusations. I was sick of living in a world where I was always on display. I wanted to hide among the shadows. Be invisible. Fuck, I wanted to be like Scarlette.

Shaking his head, Talon finally took a step away from me. "I don't know what's wrong with you, but we are family. If you want to ruin your life, then you need to just go ahead and do it," he snarled, before turning and storming away.

A few people had stopped to watch our heated exchange, but mostly, everyone went on with their days, pretending as though they weren't trying to listen to every single one of our words. Troy started to walk toward us, but after seeing me, he turned and began running the other way. Good, I hope the fucker stays away from me.

"Did you all enjoy the fucking show?" I yelled out, throwing my hands up in the air.

All eyes turned away from me. No one was stupid enough to respond to me. They just kept walking. Not even the teachers yelled at me for using profanity.

As the crowds in the hallway began to clear, I spotted a pair of eyes watching me from a distance.

Scarlette.

I stared back at her, daring her to come over to me and say something. I desperately wanted her to make the first move and come over to me.

Scarlette just stared blankly at me, like she didn't know what to do. For some strange reason, that sent a pain shooting through my body.

Shaking my head, I punched the wall as I tore my eyes away from her and then walked down the hallway and away from her sad, sad eyes.

CHAPTER 10

SCARLETTE

There were days that I completely loathed being invisible.

I was always that girl hiding in the back of the classroom. Or, the quiet kid who never dared to speak up when my parents had their business clients for dinner. I had spent the majority of my life feeling as though I didn't really exist. While I never would have admitted it to my parents or anyone else, it always brought on a great deal of sadness.

But today, being invisible was exactly what I was happy for.

As I walked through the halls of my high school, I felt the prying eyes of my classmates on me. Never before had they even noticed me. I was the ghost that walked the halls among them. Not today, though. No, today all eyes seem to be cast on me. I was the girl who had been mysteriously carried out of a party by Ason Antoni. The girl who no one really knew, but I was making waves in the small pond of my private school. Or so, I had been told by Macy.

From the moment I stepped through the doors of school today, Macy had bombarded me with all of the talk and rumors being spread. I wanted to go back to being the girl that no one cared about.

"Hey, what are you doing?" Macy asked, as she walked up to me while I was at my locker.

I had seen the exchange between Ason and Talon. Every-one had. I didn't mean to stare, but for some reason, when

Ason or the Elites were around, I couldn't tear my eyes off of them. There was something different about Ason today. I didn't know what it was, but his vibe was different.

"Nothing," I stated, slamming my locker door closed.

"Everyone is watching you," she began, her eyes narrowing on me.

I tried to act as though the attention didn't bother me, but Macy knew me too well. Rolling her eyes, Macy glanced around the crowded halls. "People are talking about what happened last weekend. They..."

Before she could finish, I held my hand up to stop her. "I don't care what people are saying. Nothing happened and I don't walk to talk about this," I stated, before storming off.

I moved through the sea of people and they all parted for me, in a way in which had never happened before.

When I walked into my class, everyone stopped talking and turned to look at me. Keeping my head down, I tried to ignore their stares, but it was hard not to notice how everyone turned their heads my way. Slumping in my seat, I made sure to not look up the rest of the class.

By the time school was over, I had practically felt like I was running from monsters.

I didn't listen to the rumors, but the hushed voices were like raging screams. The suspicious glares, the narrowed eyes, the way everyone looked at me like I was a criminal... none of it made any sense. Dread consumed me as I walked toward the library. Part of me hoped that Ason didn't show up for our tutoring session, but another part of me secretly wanted to see him. I had so many questions for him.

As I stepped inside of the library, Mrs. Miller waved me over. "Hey, I'm glad you decided to show up again," she said, laughing nervously.

I wondered if she had been a witness to the way people were treating me today. Even though Mrs. Miller had always been kind to me, she also knew that I wasn't popular at school.

"Well, I signed up to do a job," I said, shrugging.

She smiled, the creases at her eyes seeming to age her. I walked to the back room and sat down at the large table. My phone buzzed and as I pulled it out, I spotted a text from Macy.

Macy: You better tell me everything that happened last weekend!

Sighing, I typed out a text to her, knowing that she would eventually get me to spill the details.

Me: There isn't anything interesting to tell, but I will call you tonight when I get home.

Macy: I will just come over; this conversation needs to take place face-to-face.

Just as I went to type a rebuttal, a large bag fell beside me with a loud boom.

Jumping out of my skin, I let out a little scream as I turned to see Ason walk into the room. He had thrown his baseball bag next to a chair and now his metal bat was clanging against the walls of the room.

He sat down across from me, not speaking, and an angry scowl across his features. His folder sat in the center of the table. I carefully put my phone down, afraid of what to do next. I swear, Ason was like a wild animal. He was wild and dangerous and you never knew what he was going to do next. A heavy tension filled the room as we just sat there, staring at one another. His chest rose and fell rapidly as though he were out of breath.

Reaching across the table, Ason grabbed his folder and began inspecting the assignments inside. After a few minutes, I finally mustered the courage to speak.

"Do you need help with anything?" I asked, my voice barely above a whisper.

Not even bothering to look up, Ason shakes his head. "No, I don't want to bother you." He roughly ran a hand through his hair, his eyes still skimming the pages.

Frustration seeped up in me. "You aren't bothering me. This is my job. I'm here to..." before I could finish talking, Ason held up his hand to silence me.

"Whatever you have to say right now, doesn't interest me. Can we just get this over with? I have practice," he huffed, rolling his eyes as he gripped the folder tighter in his large hands.

Disrespect coming from an asshole like Ason was something I wasn't going to tolerate. I may not be popular or important around here like he his, but I am still a person and I deserve so much more than this. Especially, after he basically kidnapped me last weekend. It was because of him that people were talking about me.

"Does it make you feel good to treat people like garbage?" I asked, my anger finally reaching its boiling point. "You act like I'm the one punishing you; like I'm the one who is making you sit here with me. I know that I'm not beautiful or popular like the girls you typically having chasing after you, but I am still a person and I don't deserve this."

Tears burn my eyes and I know that I am on the brink of completely losing all of my emotions. Standing, I grab my phone and rush out of the room. As I race through the library, I shove out of the large double doors and once my feet hit the tile of the hallway, I feel the tension break and tears begin pouring down my face. I can barely see as I run, my sobs coming out rapidly. As I reach the end of the hallway,

I collapse to the ground, hugging my knees to my chest. I'm not sure why I am breaking like this. I've never cared before what people think of me. But with Ason, he has this power to destroy all of my senses.

I don't even realize that Ason had followed me until I hear his footsteps echoing down the hall. A loud sob escapes and all I want to do is crawl into a hole and die. I'm not sure how much more I can take from Ason.

"Please, just go away," I cry out, not even bothering to look up.

I have no way of knowing that it's Ason that followed me, other than that his presence seems to consume the space around me. His spicey cologne fills my nostrils and I hate myself for inhaling the intoxicating smell.

Maybe if I ignore him, he will go away? Though, I know fate hates me way too much to ever give me that kind of luck.

"Scarlette," Ason speaks, but his voice sounds different.

Rough.

Filled with remorse?

I have no idea and honestly, I don't care. I'm just ready to get out of here and never come back again. Maybe I can convince my parents to send me to a different private school. Maybe one across the country? I'm sure it wouldn't be too difficult, seeing as though they are never home and wouldn't probably miss me.

I hear him slide down the lockers that I am leaning against until he is sitting next to me. I take in a sharp breath from his nearness. My head spins and I feel sick again. Is it possible to feel drunk just from being in close contact with someone as dangerous as Ason?

"Will you talk to me?" he asks gently.

This isn't the Ason that I have gone to school with for years. Gone is the angry boy who just talked to me like I was no better than the dirt on his shoes.

I raise my head, my tear-stained cheeks burning. "Why? So you can insult me again?" My lips tremble and I go to look away.

Ason reaches out and grabs my chin, stopping my movement. The touch causes a spark to flutter through me. His gaze snapped to mine in a flash and I inhaled a deep breath. His eyes fell to my lips, causing me to blush and bite my lower lip in worry. Something about the way his breathing became heavy caused me to still under his touch.

"No, so I can fucking apologize," he says, his words almost a whisper.

Dropping his hand to his side, I scoot down from him as I attempt to compose myself. Closing his eyes, he drags a hand through his thick hair. Swallowing, I look at him as he shakes his head in contempt. Those dark eyes shoot open and I feel like he is piercing my soul with just a glance.

"Ok," is all I can muster.

His head jerks to the side and he almost looks startled that I spoke. My pulse quickened as his intense stare lingered over me again. He opened his mouth, then shut it. I could see the fury storming through his dark eyes. Why was he so complicated?

Why was this exchange so heated?

I barely knew Ason, and yet, we were almost at war with one another. And I doubt either one of us knows why.

"I'm sorry," he said in a rush.

Even though his words were harsh and quick, I felt the power behind them. I had no doubt in my mind that Ason Antoni never apologized. But for some reason, he was apologizing to me. None of this made any sense.

"It's ok," I spoke.

Honestly, I wasn't sure what to say.

"What I said wasn't ok," he gritted out. Part of me wondered if he had meant to say the words aloud. "I do stupid shit without thinking sometimes."

His words stunned me. They were raw and honest and I believed him. I had never heard Ason speak this much in all of the years that I had known him. He rubbed his knees and his knuckles almost turned white. He seemed almost angry.

I nodded, acknowledging his words. I had no idea what I was supposed to say, so I just let the silence do the talking for me.

Wiping my eyes, I knew that I needed to get up off of the floor. I had acted out of emotions and now, I was embarrassed to be seen like this. I pushed myself off of the floor and stood. Ason got up, too, and we stood in the darkened hallway. Running my hands over my pleated skirt, I offered a slight smile his way. I started to walk away, but I paused. I had to acknowledge this moment. It may be the only time Ason ever shows true kindness again.

"It's ok. I appreciate your apology," I stated, before turning on my heel to walk away.

Before I could make it down the hallway, I felt a pair of strong arms grab me. Halting my steps, my heart kicked into overdrive. Spinning around, I came face-to-face with Ason once again.

"Never let anyone disrespect you, Scarlette," he stated, with his velvety voice.

Heat rushed to my core as the sound of my name on his lips; it sounded like a sin and it was too much for me to handle. My breath caught in my throat and all I could do was stare blankly at him. I was frozen in place.

Paralyzed by his essence.

I stared at him, watching how his jaw ticked and his eyes flashed with a raging inferno. I wanted to know what he was thinking and feeling. I wanted to dive into his heart and mind; even though I knew it was insane to think anything at all about Ason.

"Why do you care?" I dared to ask.

Before I knew what was happening, Ason leaned down and crashed his lips to mine. I lost all control of my senses as I felt his lips touch mine. It was everything and more as my heart beat wildly against my chest and my body filled with a need I had never experienced before. I was caving to his touch, unable to resist him. Never in my life had anyone kissed me like this before. He fisted my hair in his hands and the pain was welcomed.

As quickly as the kiss had happened, it was over and I stepped back on wobbly legs. My hand went to my swollen mouth and shock registered as my body froze in place. Ason Antoni had just kissed me and I had let him.

His chest rose and fell rapidly as he towered over me. Wide eyes stared blankly at me, analyzing my reaction to the madness that had just happened. Sighing, he tucked a lose strand of my hair behind my ear. I couldn't move or react. I felt like I was having an out of body experience and I was just hoovering in the air, watching the scene play out.

"I'm sorry, I didn't..." he stopped mid-sentence, letting out a growl before storming away.

All I could do was just stand there and watch his back as he ran down the hallway. Shoving through the wide double doors, he disappeared outside. The slamming of the doors closing jolted me out of my stupor. My hand was still to my mouth and the lingering taste of Ason on my lips felt like a wicked prize. I had no idea what in the hell had just happened, but I knew one thing was for sure; my life would never be the same.

CHAPTER 11

ASON

"**D**amn, Ason. Are you trying to kill me?" Talon shouted out, as he caught the ball I had just thrown.

After kissing Scarlette, I had run straight to the baseball field. I still had an hour before practice started so I had called Talon and made him come here so I could get some throwing in. My anger poured of me in waves.

Throwing the glove on the ground, Talon rubbed his hand. I could see that his hand was red and starting to swell. I should feel bad, but I didn't.

"Shut up and catch the ball," I shouted.

Shaking his head, Talon started to walk toward me. I didn't want to talk to him because I feared I may admit what I had done. Kissing Scarlette was wrong and dangerous, yet it had felt like being born again. Never in my life had I felt such a rush in my life.

It was insane, because Talon and I always talked about girls. They were conquests to us and nothing more, but with Scarlette, she was something to keep as a secret. A precious prize not to be flaunted or put in the same category as all the other girls we messed around with.

"I'm not going to do anything until you tell me what in the hell is going on. I mean, you are always a mood asshole, but something is off," he said, his eyes narrowing in on me.

"Watch how you talk to me, Talon," I warned.

Talon towered over me, his broad frame blocking out the fading evening sunlight. Everyone else was terrified of Talon. Not just because of his size, but because of his rowdy behavior. He had no problem fighting or picking up something and throwing them across the field if needed. I knew though, that he would never step up to me like that. We both knew that I was possibly going to be the capo of the Antoni Mafia Family one day. No one fucked with the boss.

"Ason, you need to figure your shit out. I'm calling a meeting tonight when you get home," he announced, like he was some fucking big shot.

I went to argue with him, but to my shock and surprise, Talon walked away.

By the end of practice, I had destroyed two of our pitcher's gloves and almost broken my bat.

I had never been more thankful for the sport of baseball in all of my life. If I couldn't take out all of my anger and aggression on the field, I seriously worried that I would have killed someone by now. I mean, it was in my blood to be a killer.

When I got home, my parents were in the kitchen and I could hear the voices of my uncles, too.

"Ason, come in here," my dad announced.

Dropping my baseball bag to the floor in the foyer, I stepped into the large kitchen where my dad sat at the kitchen table with Solly, Chance, and Ryder. My mom was busy at the stove, removing a pan of baked spaghetti from the oven.

Dread consumed me as I watched them all eye me carefully. Sitting down next to my dad, I tried to keep my face as expressionless as possible.

"How was practice?" dad asked.

"It was fine," I stated, shrugging my shoulders.

Mom placed a plate in front of me and I dug in immediately, savoring the sweet scent of her homemade sauce. Garlic and herbs raced along my taste buds and I almost moaned from the pleasure of the taste.

"That's good," dad began. I could tell he was just making small talk. "We were out taking care of some business earlier, and decided tonight would be a good time to talk to you about your future," dad began.

When he said 'business' I knew that he was referring to mafia business.

Illegal guns.

Killing.

Working out of their Savannah casino night club.

I took another bite of the food, nodding along as though I were really concerned about this conversation. I knew it didn't matter what I wanted. My life had already been planned out for me before my conception. My father was in the mafia once he became my age. It was destined to be my fate. That thought had me feeling lifeless.

Smacking my back, Chance laughed. "Come on, kid. Don't look so worried. We aren't going to ask you to wack anyone just yet."

My head snapped to the side as I glared at Chance. He thought all of this shit was funny. Chance and my dad both grew up in this lifestyle, while Ryder and Solly begged, pleaded, and did anything they could to find a spot in the mafia.

"Funny," I mumbled.

"We have several opportunities for you, Ason. We just want you to start thinking about which role in the Antoni Mafia you would like to partake in," Solly noted, his serious tone changing the atmosphere in the room.

As always, my dad just sat back and watched our exchanges. He was a man of few words, but I guess he could get away with that as the capo. Sometimes, I liked to think I was like him...

"Just think about it. Maybe even spend a day with one of us. Get your feet wet," Ryder added.

"Ok. Well, I will have to look at my schedule. With school, baseball, and now these fucking tutoring sessions..."

"Watch your mouth," mom shouted across the kitchen.

"Sorry," I grumbled out.

It was hilarious when they tried to parent me. My parents talked worse than anyone I had ever met, but God forbid I utter a curse word, too.

I finished eating while the men around me talked about work and what they thought might be best for me. I knew this was far different from how my dad made his way into the mafia, but still, none of it felt right to me. I loved the idea of being powerful, but I wasn't sure if I was willing to kill for it.

CHAPTER 12

SCARLETTE

The rest of the week flew by without any more incidents. Ason and I didn't have any more tutoring sessions until next week. It was Friday and Macy wanted me to go to another party with her. After my last experience, I wasn't ready to show my face at any more parties. I decided to instead spend the weekend alone. My parents were gone again. My dad had a business conference in Destin, Florida, so my mom went with him.

Of course, they left me home alone with a credit card to spend on food and necessities. Part of me wished they would have taken me with them, but I knew that was just wishful thinking.

Stepping into Dodd's Bakery, I took in the sweet scent of freshly baked muffins and cakes. While the bakery was located at the riverfront walkway, a good few miles away from my house, it was my favorite and I knew eating sweets all weekend would make me feel better.

My phone pinged in my pocket as I walked up to the counter.

Macy: Are you home?

Me: No.

Macy: Are you going to Sarah's party with me?

I had already declined her offer, but Macy thought that she could persuade me to go anyway.

I saw the little bubbles dancing across the screen and I almost laughed while I waited in line to order. The glass case displayed rows of scrumptious of homemade cookies, muffins, and other pastries that had my mouth watering with just a glance.

Macy: Come on, Scarlette. I promise I won't let you drink this time. Besides, what are you doing anyway?

Me: I'm out and I have plans tonight.

I tucked my phone back into my blazer pocket. I was still wearing my school uniform and hadn't bothered to go home and change after school. I didn't need to try and explain to Macy what my plans were. She didn't need to know that my real plans were to lay around all weekend watching old movies on Netflix while stuffing my face with sweets. I knew how much of a loser I sounded like, but I didn't care. The thought of running into Ason again had me wanting to hide out all weekend. And, that was exactly what I planned on doing.

Once it was my turn to order, I purchased a large box of assorted treats. Turning to leave, I walked back outside and allowed the glowing sun and slight wind from the water to greet me. Walking along the river walk was calming. There were so many fantastic restaurants, boutique shops, and bakeries that people loved to visit. Down further was the old River Front Casino where my father visited every so often when he was entertaining clients that came to town.

Since I didn't have anywhere to be, I decided to enjoy the stroll along the sidewalk. The water splashed along the bank and the soft melody of an acoustic guitar sang in the air as a man strummed along on a bench. I was busy watching him play and not paying attention to where I was going. Suddenly, felt my body colliding with a large, strong frame.

"I'm so sorry," I rushed out an apology, as I dared to look up.

My eyes locked with Ason's and a gasp slipped past my lips. I had spent all week trying to avoid him and I run into him here!

"Thought you were trying to avoid me," he stated. It sounded more like an accusation, rather than an observation.

His blue eyes were piercing through me as he ran a hand roughly through his dark hair. Like me, he still wore his school uniform, but on him, it looked amazing.

Gazing up at him, I held tightly to the pink box that held my treats—I mean, my weekend plans. Nerves consumed me and I wasn't sure how to react to him. He wasn't wrong; I had been avoiding him and that was exactly why I didn't go to the party with Macy.

"What are you doing here?" I blurted out.

Chuckling, Ason looked away for a second before turning back to face me again. "I thought this was a public place," he responded. The smirk playing on his lips did things to me that it shouldn't.

"It is, I just assumed that you would..." my words were cut off.

"What? That I would be partying and getting drunk and high? You think that I go around wreaking havoc and killing people?" he shouted, his nostrils flaring as his words sliced through me.

White hot tears blinded me as hurt tore through me like a raging tornado. Once again, I had let Ason Antoni, a guy who I barely knew, cause me pain and embarrassment. My hands shook and I dropped the box filled with the treats I had just purchased. I hadn't accused him of anything and it seemed like he was taking his own guilt and insecurities out on me.

"If you had let me talk and not cut me off, you would have heard me say that I just assumed that you would be out with friends—and not alone. But since you love to torture me, I see that is what you are really doing here," I cried, shoving past him as I began to race down the sidewalk.

My SUV was parked a few blocks away and I ran as fast as I could, praying I could get there before I lost all sanity. I hated Ason Antoni with all of my being. He was cocky, arrogant, and cruel. I was nothing more to him than a peasant that he could ridicule and hurt just because he could. People shouted for me to slow down as I sprinted forward. I didn't bother to listen to anyone. I had to get to my car and the hell away from this place. What had become a great start to my weekend, had just turned into hell.

Finding my SUV, I sed through downtown Savannah and back to my secluded subdivision. Passing through the gates that separated my neighborhood from the rest of Savannah, I drove to my house. Passing by perfectly manicured lawns and houses that resembled castles, I sped like I was in the Indy 500. Once I was safely back in my house, I wiped the tears away and fell onto the large, white sofa in our family room.

Family room, that was hilarious. This room was cold and stuffy and never housed a real family. I felt resentment bubbling up inside of me as I thought about how lonely I was. My parents, who I knew deep down loved me, also neglected me. They bought me presents as a way to show love, but what I really wanted was their time and affection. Though, I would never say that to them aloud.

Closing my eyes, I counted to ten inside of my head as I willed myself to calm down. Suddenly, a bang on the front door startled me. I knew it was probably Macy and I wasn't in the mood to deal with her theatrics right now. Deciding to ignore the knock, I pushed myself off the couch and decided to just go upstairs. As I walked toward the spiral staircase, the knocking on the front door grew louder and more intense.

Huffing, I went to the front door and as I pulled the door open, I was shocked when standing on my front porch was Ason Antoni and not Macy.

He looked out of place standing on my stoop. His intense glare only petrified me more. I went to slam the door in his face, but he put his foot out, blocking me from shutting the door.

"Wait, you forgot something," he said, handing me the pink box I had dropped back at the river front.

My anger quieted for a brief moment as I stared down at the box in his hands. Taking the box, I offered a slight smile.

"Thank you," I whispered.

Nodding, Ason shoved his hands in his perfectly ironed khaki pants. "I wanted to also say that I am sorry if I scared you," he said, shocking me even more. "When you started to talk, I thought you were going to bring up some rumor or something. Everyone outside of my group of friends gossips about me. I thought you might do the same and think I was doing something..." He stops, shaking his head. "It doesn't matter what. I just need to watch how I react."

My eyes bulged as I leaned in closer to make sure I had heard him correctly.

"It's ok." I feel a ball of nervous energy transpire between us. "I yelled back at you and then ran off like a crazy person," I say, trying to lighten the mood.

Ason's flashy car sits in my driveway and I glance around to see if any of the neighbor's notice. Thankfully, no one seems to be outside right now.

"Yeah, well, I'm still sorry," he grumbles out. "So, what's in the box?" he asks, as I awkwardly hold the box in my hands.

"It's an arrangement of sweets from Dodds Bakery," I tell him.

"Oh, I have always wondered what they have in there," he says, shrugging his shoulders.

"You've never had one of their chocolate chunk cookies? Or, their award-winning cupcakes?" I practically yell out.

That elicits a laugh from Ason. His eyes almost sparkle as a smile forms over his lips. "Nah, I'm not really into sweets. They smell good, though," he finishes, nodding his head toward the box.

"Why don't you come in and try something. I mean, you came all the way to my house to apologize and bring me back the box I dropped," I offer.

I don't bother mentioning the fact that he yelled at me, once again, in public. That seems irrelevant right now.

"Are you sure?" he asks. I can see the hesitation on his face.

"Yeah, why not? I'm your tutor and the least I can do right now is give you one of Dodd's amazing treats since you are basically being punished to do school work with me for an hour a week," I laugh.

"It's not a punishment," he says so low, I barely hear him.

I turn and move out of the doorway and Ason steps inside of my house. I feel the energy in the foyer shift by his presence alone. Other than Macy, no one from my school has ever stepped foot inside of my house before. Especially, not an Elite.

Closing the door behind me, we begin walking down the hallway toward the kitchen. I place the pink box on the white marble counter and slowly remove the lid. Inside, all of my delicious treats are calling to me. Ason stands a few feet away from me, watching me with a fierce look.

I pull out two of the massive chocolate chunk cookies. Handing one to Ason, he accepts the gift.

Taking a bite, I close my eyes and allow the sweet chocolate and buttery goodness of the soft cookie to please my taste buds.

Ason takes a small bite and then I hear him moan. "Wow, this really is good," he acknowledges.

"I told you. These are my favorites. I went and got an entire box to last me the entire weekend," I let slip. Cringing, I hate that I just told him that.

Man, Ason is going to think that I am a complete loser now. Who buys a box of cookies and cupcakes to enjoy all weekend? A girl with no social life, that's who. Ason takes another bite and then swallows. Watching him eat the cookie is almost a turn on. I never thought something so simple could be so hot.

"You were right. So, am I keeping you from something?" he asks, glancing around the empty room.

Shaking my head, I feel that twinge of pain again. "No. My parents are gone again for the weekend and Macy is at a party.

You are looking at my weekend plans," I say, pointing to the baked goods.

I don't dare to look at him, so I keep my eyes trained on the remainder of the cookie in my hand.

"I wish I could just do nothing on the weekends," Ason states flatly. "I was at the river front doing some...work with one of my uncles," he says suspiciously. But I don't press that matter. "Doing nothing sounds great."

"Yeah, I'm sure," I mock, rolling my eyes.

He's obviously making fun of me or trying to pity me. I must sound like such a freak to him.

"No, I'm serious," Ason says, he places the cookie on the counter and looks at me sincerely. "It must be nice to just relax"

The longing in his voice makes me almost feel sorry for him. There's a sadness in his eyes that makes me want to reach out and hug him, but thankfully, I don't.

"It is, but..." I go to say something, but then stop myself.

I'm not sure why I feel compelled to tell him anything about myself or honest feelings. For a moment, Ason almost appears as a regular guy. Our conversation feels light and easy, but I quickly remind myself that Ason is an Elite. The son of a mafia mob boss and a very powerful guy. He's not my friend.

"What?" he asks, narrowing his gaze on me.

Shaking my head, I wave my hand in the air, dismissing the idea. "Nothing, it's silly."

"No, say what you were going to say. This is one of the first conversations I've had in a long time that hasn't made me want to scream or punch someone," he states.

That causes me to giggle. I imagine Ason and the rest of the rowdy Elites sitting around and talking. I'm sure their conversations are as wild as their reputations.

"Well, I was just going to say that it is nice to have the house all to myself, but sometimes I wish that it wasn't so lonely," I admit.

Heat creeps to my cheeks as I blush. I have no idea what it is about Ason right now, but something about the way he is looking at me is causing me to become flustered. Honesty is pouring out of me in waves and I can't stop the explosion.

"That's funny, because I would love to be alone. I feel like I am always surrounded by people," Ason tells me. His eyes grow large, as though he didn't expect to say those words to me. It's funny how two opposite strangers are having a heart-to-heart conversation right now. "Wow, this just got deep," he chuckles.

"Yeah, it must be the cookies," I laugh.

We stand there for a few more minutes before his phone buzzes from his pocket. Sighing, Ason almost looks angry by the interruption. I'm sure that I was just imagining that. I'm sure he would rather be anywhere else but here with me. Pulling out his phone, Ason rolls his eyes as he glances down at his phone. Running a hand roughly through his hair, he quickly types out a response then shoves the phone back inside his pocket.

"I have to leave, but this was...nice," he finishes.

"Yeah. I'm sorry that I kept you so long," I instantly start apologizing.

"It was nice." Ason turns to leave and I follow him to the front door.

He turns and I bump into his hard chest. The urge to run my hands along his perfectly sculpted abs overwhelms me. Ason meets my stare and he tenses. Cupping my face with his hands, he leans in and places a soft kiss to my lips. The movement is a surprise and I am so startled it takes me a moment to respond. His tongue runs along my bottom lip before entering my mouth. He tastes like a mixture of mint and smoke and strangely enough, the taste is intoxicating. After a few more seconds, the kiss softens and we both give in. My body relaxes and I hear Ason release a slight sigh. His other hand slides up my side and caresses my sensitive skin. I feel myself growing wet and this is a new sensation for me. No guy has ever made me feel this way before.

When he tears his mouth away from me, I feel a yearning to pull him back to me.

"I should leave, but I can't," he growls out.

Hesitating, my mind is racing and I am not sure what to do. We are alone in my house and my body is craving for more of his touch. His hand on my waist reminds me that I've never been touched like this before. Damn, I am so pathetic. Ason must be so experienced with other girls. What if I am a bad kisser? Or, I don't know what to do to please him? Sensing my unease, Ason begins to rub my back gently.

"It's ok if you don't want this. I just...had to try, at least once. I had to taste and feel you at least once," he says.

There is something about the way his words ignite my soul that has me lusting for more of him. He wants to taste and feel me? How long has he thought about this? The problem with this is that Ason and I come from very different worlds. One where he is important and one where I am—not.

I stare up at him, unsure of what to do. "I'm just a nobody," I say.

Anger flares across his face and I try to step back, but Ason stops me. Pulling me to him, he stuns me with another kiss. However, this kiss isn't soft and sweet. No, this one is hungry and needy and tells me that he wants me. "Don't you ever say that you are a nobody again," he says into my mouth.

Unable to speak, I kiss him back, thrusting my hands into his wild hair. For a moment, we are nothing but hands and kisses and this is the most exciting thing that has ever happened to me. His phone chimes and he let out a frustrated sigh. Releasing me, he huffs as he looks conflicted.

"I have to go, but I want to do this again," he says, and I know he means more than just hanging out and eating sweets.

"I want to do it again, too," I say, breathlessly.

Opening the door, he walks outside and I notice the sun is fading over the horizon. The sky is painted with reds and purples and I take a second to admire the scene.

Ason walks to his car and as he opens the car door, he stops and a strange expression crosses his features. He almost looks torn. I stand in the doorway, watching him. Offering a slight wave, I go to close the door as he slides into the driver's seat. The roar of his engine rocks me to my core. He speeds down the road and I can't stop staring until his taillights fade and only silence is left behind.

Slamming the front door closed, I lean against the large frame and exhale a deep breath. Ason Antoni was just in my house. Talking to me like we were old friends. An Elite, sitting with me. Kissing me and blowing my mind with revelations that I still am not sure are true or not. It was so absurd; it was almost surreal. What in the hell just happened?

CHAPTER 13

ASON

Pressing the accelerator down to the floor, I feel my car jump forward.

Taking the old backroads to my family home allows me to drive recklessly. Right now, I need to feel reckless. After Scarlette had run off from the river front, all logical thinking went away. I followed her back to her house. I knew it was wrong and I shouldn't, but I honestly felt bad for hurting her feelings. Plus, she had dropped the ten-pound box of baked goods and I didn't know if she needed them for something important.

The last thing I had expected was for Scarlette to invite me into her house. Being there with her was strange, but at the same time, it felt right. Like I was going home for the first time after a long trip. I saw a different side of her in those few minutes we spent alone, but then an emergency text from Micah had ruined that short-lived bliss I had felt. I could still taste her sweet lips and her lavender scent floated through my car. Kissing Scarlette had been something I had dreamed about for years. Now that I had had my chance to taste her, I knew she was a drug that I would never be able to kick. I wanted more from her, but I also knew that Scarlette wasn't the type of girl to just fuck after a few times hanging out. She wasn't like the usual girls I hooked up with. She was special.

I punched in his name on the speed dial connected to my car and waited for him to answer.

"Where are you?" his deep voice asked over the speakers.

Gripping the steering wheel tighter, I took a sharp turn that had my car almost on its side. "On my way home."

"We are waiting for you down by the swamps," he stated, and that was when I could hear the sounds of the rest of our crew in the background.

I hung up the call, not wanting to talk right now. I took a right and then went through the gates to our driveway. Instead of taking the driveway to the main house, I turned down the dirt side road that led behind the house and toward the swamps at the back of our property. It was in these very same swamps where my father dumped bodies of those that dared to mess with the mafia. A shudder tore through me as I thought about that. As a kid, I would ride my bike to the swamps whenever I saw my dad or uncles make their way down that road. I would hide out among the tall grass and trees, watching the deadly exchanges take place. At first, witnessing brutal acts by the men who I had looked up to had terrified me. But over the years, I had grown accustomed to the evil and vile acts of my lifestyle. Watching bodies drop into the murky water, only to hear the splash and growls of the alligators as they ripped the bodies apart—only brought on nightmares in my childhood.

As I approached the swamps, the sun was gone and in its place was a silent and eerie darkness. The glowing lights of cars seeped through the trees as I parked. Everyone was already waiting for me, standing around and talking. Talon had a beer in his hand and Gabby was focused in on her phone.

"Look who finally decided to show up. Where were you?" Talon called out.

"Out," was all I said.

Moving next to Micah, I glanced around our circle. Everyone glared back at me and I didn't like the vibe of the night.

"Why are you being so secretive?" Gabby asks, finally looking up from her phone.

"I'm not, I just don't feel the need to tell you assholes where I am at all times," I said.

"Whatever, but you are a terrible liar," Gabby retorts, rolling her eyes.

Chuckling, Talon turned to me again. "Anyway," he says, waving his hands between us. "We called this meeting tonight because we need to know what your plans are for us." His eyes bore into mine and I hated how they were acting just like our parents. Desperately I wished that we could just be teenagers. A group of friends who hung out and got into trouble, and not the prodigies of the mafia.

"I went earlier today to meet up with Ryder at the casino," I state flatly. My eyes dance over to Micah and he stands there smugly, his blue eyes glowing against the blackness of the night. "I haven't made a decision yet, but that's my business right now. I still have time," I finish, kicking the dirt beneath me.

An internal clock slowly ticks away at me each and every single day. I am reminded constantly that my fate is counting down to the moment when I must decide what role I want to take in the Antoni Mafia Family. More than anything, I want to scream at them all to just fuck off, but I know that I can't. I'm expected to be the next capo. To lead my unruly family through the mafia world. It makes me want to throw up.

"My parents worked hard to establish that casino. If you aren't serious about it, you need to back off," Micah warns, and I don't like the tone of his voice or the way he is glaring at me.

Stepping toward him, my fists beg to unleash against his face. We don't fight amongst one another. We are a solid family, but right now, I am on a short fuse and anything may just set me off.

Talon steps in to stop me. "Ason, you need to calm down. Besides, Micah has a point. It would make more sense for

Micah to take on the nightclubs and casinos. People would question his role there less knowing that his mother inherited the casino from her father and his father started the nightclub shortly after that."

"Hey, can we wrap this up? I have plans tonight," Gabby cuts in.

We all turn to look at her. Gabby knows that her role in the Antoni Mafia Family will more than likely be as one of our snipers or assassins. Her mother, Gia, is one of the best shooters I know. Well, besides Ryder. Our arguments over our places seem irrelevant to her and I guess in a way, she's right.

"Yeah, I've got about five chicks waiting for me. You all coming to Tucker's Lake house? He's got a DJ and keg set up," Talon says, dropping his hands and completely forgetting that he almost had to break up a fight.

"I'm in," Micah says, pumping his fist in the air.

"That's where I am going, just ride with me," Gabby offers, starting to walk toward her sleek Mercedes convertible.

"Nah, I think I am just going to go home," I say, pretending to yawn.

"No, you are coming out with us," Talon says, throwing an arm around my shoulder.

As he leads me to the car, I exhale a deep breath because I know I can't get out of this now.

An hour later, I am sitting on a brown leather couch in what looks more like a resort, rather than a lake house. Music fills into the house through open windows as a DJ is set-up out on the large deck that overlooks the lake. People drink and dance all around me. A couple of guys pass around a joint in the kitchen.

I sit nursing my beer and counting down the minutes until we can leave. Everyone around me is trashed, except for Gabby. She had one rough night after drinking way too much, and she hasn't had a drop since.

She's busy dancing on the patio with a few girls who she dances with on the dance team. They throw their hands up in the air like they have no cares in the world.

"Hey, Ason," Tara Jones says, as she sidles up next to me on the couch.

Her bleach blonde hair flows down her back and her drunken eyes drink me in. She smells like tequila and roses and the scent is almost unbearable. She rubs her leg against mine and I notice that her skin tight white dress barely covers her ass.

"Hey," I offer, not bothering to look at her.

She pats my shoulder as she leans in closer. She's well past drunk right now and acting sloppy. "Want to go upstairs?" she asks, her words starting to slur.

"Nope. I'm all good," I say, taking a drink of my beer.

Her hair brushes against my neck and the sensation almost have me jumping off this sofa. "Come on, I'll suck you off," she offers, batting her fake lashes at me.

Shaking my head, I throw back the remainder of my beer and then push Tara off of me. Storming through the kitchen, I inhaled a hard breath. A few people I passed tried to talk to me, but I kept walking. I found the laundry room and decided to hide out in there for a little while.

My phone began blowing up with texts and calls, but I just ignored them all. The last thing I wanted to do right now was talk to anyone. I felt my pulse kick as images of Scarlette flew through my mind. More than anything, I wished that I could be sitting with her at her house. Talking about nothing at all while eating those ridiculous cookies. The thumping of the music mixed with the beer and stale stench of weed was giving me a headache. A nice, quiet night at home sounded really nice.

A pounding on the door rocked me and I swung the door open. "What the hell, man?" Talon asked, a girl hanging off his arm.

"What are you doing?" I asked, watching the girl nibble on his ear.

"Dude, this girl wants me, but all of the rooms upstairs are occupied. Can I use the room after you?" he asked, leaning into the room and glancing around for what I assume was a girl. "Wait, are you in here alone?" he asked, narrowing his eyes at me.

I moved my hand from the doorknob and shoved past him. "It's all yours," I grumbled, moving past them.

Talon yelled out a thanks before I heard the door slam and giggling ensued. Shaking my head, I moved back to the kitchen. Most of the people were now outside or in the living room. Leaning against the black granite countertop, I looked around for any signs of Gabby or Micah. I was ready to get the hell out of here.

Suddenly, I felt a pair of eyes on me. Tara was sauntering toward me, a smirk playing on her lips. Damn, this girl can't take a hint. I try not to give her any attention, but she doesn't seem to notice. Tara has been after the Elites for years. She has slept with Talon and sucked Micha's dick. I knew she was after me, too, and normally, I wouldn't think twice about banging her. However, the thought of hooking up with some power-hungry slut like Tara, just doesn't feel right.

"Where did you go?" she asks, sliding next to me.

"I wanted some privacy," I tell her, hoping for once she will take the hint.

Smiling, she leans in and brushes her hand against my forearm. Her fliting does nothing for me and I desperately want to run away from here. It terrifies me that the only place I want to escape to right now is Scarlette's house.

"That sounds fun. How about we go upstairs and look for an empty room?" she asks, licking her lips suggestively.

Tara presses her body against mine, taking her hands and raking them down my chest. I see a few people pulling out their phones, ready to get a good shot of me and Tara. I'm sure they expect some X-rated show, but that's not what I am feeling tonight.

Grabbing her hands, I shove her off of me and Tara let's out a yell as she stumbles backward.

"What is wrong with you, Ason? You've never turned down pussy before," she hisses out.

A few people crowd around us, still watching the scene playout. I hate how everyone feels like they have a right to watch me. To listen to my arguments. They don't even see me as a real person.

Fuming and tired of all of this bullshit, I slam my hands down on the cool counter. "Nothing is wrong with me, you dumb bitch. Maybe I don't want to hook-up with someone as desperate and easy as you," I yell out, my rage exploding like a volcano.

Tara looks as though I have physically assaulted her. A sob escapes from her pouting lips as she runs from the room. I don't feel bad for what I said. I meant every damn word. The world was full of girls like her. Ready and willing to use their body as a weapon to get a guy like me. I didn't want that anymore.

I stood there for a moment until I heard a familiar voice break though my anger-fueled trance.

"Ason, I think it's time to leave," Gabby says, walking up to me.

Nodding, I push myself away from the counter and follow her outside. As we head to the car, I stare up at the night sky. The stars shine down brightly and I wish more than ever that I could just soar up into the vast sky and be part of those shining balls of fire.

Gabby unlocks her car and I slide into the passenger seat. I feel a headache coming on and I begin rubbing my temples. As Gabby goes to start the ignition, she pauses and turns to face me.

"Ason, I wish you would talk to me," she sighs. "You are the one we look up to. The one we all admire and aspire to be one day. But you need to let us in," she says, her voice breaking.

I turn to face her. Gabby may be one of the toughest girls I know, but underneath her armor of toughness, she has a solid heart of gold. She loves those around her fiercely and I have always admired that about her.

Part of me wants to lash out again and tell her to mind her fucking business, but I just can't. I'm too exhausted from running from myself and my family.

"Gabby, my head and heart are at war right now," I admit to her. I know my words are vague, but it's a start.

She offers a slight smile. We back out of the long driveway and begin heading toward my house. The soft melody of music plays through the speakers and for a few minutes, neither of us speaks. I am thankful for the silence, but knowing Gabby, it won't last long. When she finally speaks again, she shocks me.

"Well, if it's about Scarlette, then I think you need to let down your guard. I know she isn't one of us," she says, meaning the Elites.

I have no idea how she knows that I'm thinking about Scarlette. I haven't spoken a word about her to anyone. This new admission causes my heart to still and sweat to bead over my forehead.

"Gabby, it's not like that," I begin to lie, but she stops me.

The car slows to a stop as a redlight gleams before us. She turns and stared at me and I watch as the flashing lights of the city around us dance across her features. "Ason, please don't like to me. You and I are closer to than anyone else. I see the way you look at Scarlette. You have longed for her for years, yet you have never spoken to her until recently."

Once again, I'm thrown by her words. How in the hell did Gabby know how I felt about Scarlette. For years, I have struggled with keeping my feelings for Scarlette a secret. Wanting her and keeping her at a distance was always my inner demon. Conflicting feelings crossed over me.

"I can't have her," I whispered.

Shaking her head, Gabby laughed. "Ason, why do you feel like that? Look at our families. None of them technically should have been together, but love conquered over everything else."

Chuckling, I stared back at Gabby. I had been so lost in my own emotions and fears for so long, that I hadn't noticed that my feisty best friend had grown up. I was proud of the woman she was becoming.

"Wow, I'm impressed, Gabby. You are pretty smart," I say, causing her to smirk.

"Of course, I am. But seriously, Ason. Don't let yourself be miserable because you are afraid to go after what you want. And... if you don't want to be our capo, that's ok, too," she finishes, then clamps her mouth closed.

"I don't have a choice. My father is the Capo. It's my fate," I explain, glancing out the window as the light turns green and we continue driving.

Clutching the steering wheel, Gabby stares forward as she goes to speak. "I see how uncomfortable you get when anyone brings up you becoming the Antoni Mafia Family capo. The rest of us would die for that role, but you seem almost afraid of it," she tells me.

If this had been anyone else daring to be so brutally honest with me, I would have told them to shut the fuck up by now or jumped out of the car. But with Gabby, she knew that she could say anything she wanted to me. Not because she was a girl and I knew better than to ever hit a woman, but because she knew me better than anyone else.

"I just don't know what I want yet. I know that my life will always be the Antoni Mafia Family, but the role I play in the mafia is what I am uncertain about," I bluntly say.

"Just don't give up on us. Regardless of the role you play, we will always have your back," she states with finality.

In less than ten minutes, Gabby had broken down the walls I had spent seventeen years building. As each piece crumbled, I could feel my heart warming up to the idea that maybe, just maybe things may work out for me after all.

Chapter 14

Scarlette

"**G**irl, have you heard the news?" Macy shouts through the phone.

I hold my cellphone out as her loud screech hurts my hears.

"What are you talking about?" I ask, as I roll over in my bed.

I had spent most of the weekend in bed, watching Netflix and eating my weight in cookies and muffins. My parents had called late last night to tell me that they would be home sometime on Monday. Being alone was my norm, but it still ached to know that I was all by myself in this large house. I could have asked Macy to come over, but she would have talked me into going to some wild party with her. I just didn't feel up to being out, so walloping in my own self-pity was the plan. Plus, I still hadn't told Macy about my kiss with Ason. There was even a part of me that wondered if I had dreamed the whole thing. To think that Ason, an Elite, would ever be interested in me, blew my mind. We had hooked up, but there was no ties binding us together. We were both single, but it was complicated.

"Hold on, I will send you the video," she says, and I hear her rustling around.

"What video?" I ask, pausing the rerun episode of One Tree Hill.

My phone beeps as a message comes through. I click on the video to see Ason standing in a large kitchen, anger plastered over his face. But what catches my eye more than anything is the gorgeous, tall blonde that has her hands all over Ason's body. I recognize her from school. Her name is Tara and she is a cheerleader. Jealousy mixed with a scathing irritation races through me. I'm so glad that Macy can't see my face right now. My mouth hangs open and my body heats. Rap music and voices blend together in the background. A guy laughs and a girl whispers about how Tara has been talking all night about hooking up with Ason. My eyes can't turn away from the video and just when I think I can't watch anymore, my eyes almost bulge out of my head when Ason expectantly shoves Tara away from himself. Tara scoffs as she starts to cry. I can tell how embarrassed she must be and the crowd around them laughs as she races out of the room. The video ends and I have to stop myself from screaming out with frustration.

"What happened next?" I blurt out, before I remember that Macy is still on the phone. My heart races and I try to tame down the jealousy I feel spiking inside of me.

"From what I hear, Ason left with Gabby right after that. But people are talking..." she trails off.

"What are people saying?" I rush out. Patience is long gone and I am desperate to hear the gossip surrounding Ason.

Knowing I have no business asking anything about Ason doesn't seem to affect me. I am nothing to him, but still, I can't help but feel this dire need to know. What happened between us was hot and unexpected, but we didn't have a label.

A light giggle escapes from Macy. "Wow, I've never known you to care about school gossip," she says.

Crap. I need to come up with something so Macy doesn't start to suspect that I am interested to know things about Ason. He's savage, cruel, and powerful, but I saw another side to him that keeps me engaged.

"I'm bored," I respond. "I don't really care, but now that I've seen the video you have me interested."

"Anyway, the rumor is that Ason has some secret girl. No one knows who she is, but it must be serious if it has Ason turning down getting laid," she laughs.

I cringe as she mentions Ason hooking up with other girls. It's not a secret that he and the Elites can get anyone they want, whenever they want, but for some reason, that knowledge elevates me to another level of annoyance and hurt.

"Wow, that's interesting. Who knew the Elites would ever care for anyone but themselves," I snap.

My snarky attitude slips out, but I don't care.

"Well, I wonder who it is. Maybe it's some model or celebrity?" Macy guesses.

"Maybe," I mutter.

We talk a few more minutes before I end the call. All I can do the rest of the evening is to wonder who the mystery woman is that has captivated Ason.

Monday morning, I find myself dreading school.

Not only do I have my scheduled tutoring session with Ason, but the school is buzzing over the pep rally that will take place the second half of the day. The baseball team has a big game coming up this weekend and the basketball team is in a tournament in Charleston. The cheerleaders bounce past me as they try and hype up the students in the halls.

I avoid them most of the day, but the excitement in the school is hard to ignore. By the time the pep rally is ready to begin, I take my time putting my books in my locker as everyone else rushes to the large gymnasium.

"Scarlette, let's see if we can get good seats," Macy calls out to me.

She's walking with a few other girls, but I wave her off. "Go ahead. I will meet you there," I yell back.

Macy smiles and waves as she continues down the hallway. Maybe if I stay behind, I can sneak into the library and hide out while the rest of the school goes to the pep rally.

Realizing that sounds better than watching the cheerleaders and dance teams perform their raunchy routines for the sports teams, I go at a snail's pace finishing up at my locker. Once the halls at clear and silent, I let out a heavy breath. Looking all around, I make sure there isn't anyone around to catch me as I turn in the opposite direction of the gymnasium and toward the library. Feeling like a spy, I am careful to stay close to the pristine white walls while I pad down the hallway. Just as I reach the entrance doors to the library, I hear a deep voice that causes my heart to still and my body to shake.

"What are you doing?" Ason asks from behind me.

Stilling, I slowly turn around and lock eyes with Ason. He's delicious looking in his dark blazer and perfectly styled pants. His hair is messy and I can't help but suck in a deep breath when he runs a hand through his messy locks. His dark eyes seem to heat me to the core.

"Um..." I begin to get flustered. "I was going to check on something in the library really quick," I lie.

Shaking his head, Ason smirks and I swear, I may just die right there. He is so good looking, it's almost a sin.

"You are skipping the pep rally, aren't you?" he asks. There's a light of excitement in those dangerous eyes and I can't help but be transfixed by them.

I can't lie to him. "Yeah, it's just not for me. But, why aren't you there?" I ask, suddenly realizing he's missing his own pep rally. "You're on the baseball team."

Ason glances away for a moment like he is conflicted about what to say. It strikes me again that Ason is rumored to have a mystery girl that he has fallen for. I have no business to be talking to him right now in this darkened hallway.

"Yeah, but I don't give a shit about pep rallies. I like playing baseball, but I don't need the celebrations and nonsense that this pretentious school offers. This is just a reason for the cheerleaders and dance team to shake their asses and for students to get out of class the rest of the day," he snarls, his hostility toward the event ringing loud and clear.

"That's very... honest," I reply, not sure what else to say.

Taking a step closer, Ason paralyzes me with his smile. "Do you want to leave?" he asks.

My brain goes fuzzy and I feel like I'm in the Twilight Zone. Did I just hear him correctly?

"What?" I ask, unsure that I heard him right. Maybe my mind is playing tricks on me.

"I don't want to be here. Do you want to leave? Maybe go somewhere and get something to eat? Or, we could go ahead and get our tutoring out of the way so you don't have to stay after school today," he offers.

My heart sinks a little as he brings up our tutoring session. For just a brief second, I thought maybe, just maybe he may want to just hang out with me. Such a foolish thought for a girl like me. I'm not part of the Elite. I'm not some beautiful, runway model that he would chase after. No, I'm just plain ol' nerdy me. The girl without a life. The girl from the shadows.

"Won't your girlfriend be upset?" I ask, daring to get the answer to the gossip spreading around school.

Also, I need the confirmation for my own sanity. Knowing for sure that he has a girlfriend will help me stop this delusion I'm stuck inside of. I have to stop thinking of Ason as anything but an Elite. A powerful guy who comes from one of the most notorious families in Savannah. I need to be reminded that a guy like Ason would never look at me as anything more than a tutor. Plus, I have to know for sure if I crossed a line that I shouldn't. I would never mess around with someone else's boyfriend; regardless of how irresistible they are.

Ason's eyes narrow down at me and his mouth falls into a grim line. "I don't have a girlfriend," he states flatly.

"Oh," is all I can say.

I glance down at my shoes. I've never skipped school before, but the idea of leaving with Ason is driving me wild.

"Won't we get into trouble?" I ask, looking back up at Ason.

He's intently watching me and it makes my heart still. I can't make out his expression, but he's driving me wild.

"Who is going to tell on us? The entire school is at the pep rally," he says, that charming smile chipping away at any unease I'm feeling. "So, are you coming with me or not?" he asks, turning to walk away.

This is insane.

Ludicrous even.

But that doesn't stop me from blurting out the last thing I ever thought I would say. "Ok, sure."

"Ok, let's go," he says, leading me down the hallway.

I glance back at the empty library and then back to the strong, gorgeous boy who I am blindly following. I have no idea where we are going and right now, I honestly don't care. As I fall into step next to Ason, I feel a slight smile tug at my lips. When we exit the school, the blinding sunlight warms my already heated face. Ason leads me to toward his sleek sports car and I pause. As he goes to open his door, he notices that I have stopped.

"What?" he asks, confused.

I bite my lip and fidget with the hem of my skirt. "Do you want me to follow you in my car?"

I'm not sure he will feel awkward or embarrassed if someone were to see me with him. Of course, they would have to probably do a double take to ensure they were seeing things correctly. The Elites don't usually talk to people outside of their small, inner circle, unless they are at parties.

"No, just ride with me," he says, sliding into his driver's seat.

As I walk toward the car, I feel butterflies fluttering in my belly. This can't be real. Any minute now, I will wake up from this berserk dream. However, right now, I am going to enjoy this moment while it lasts. Sitting down next to Ason, he revs the engine as he smiles my way. My heart beats wildly against my chest as the seat below me vibrates from the massive engine running. That smile melts hearts and steals souls and right now, I have just become a victim to Ason's charm. All I can do is pray that this savage boy doesn't destroy me.

CHAPTER 15

ASON

"*Won't we get into trouble?*"

Scarlette's innocent drives me absolutely crazy. Her fear of getting into trouble only made me want her more. I knew it was wrong of me to even insist that she skip the pep rally, but I could tell that she wanted to be anywhere else but at the school. I had been watching her all day. Maintaining a healthy distance was key, but I always had a view of her. When everyone else started to make their way down to the gym, Scarlette looked around before retreating the opposite direction. Intrigued, I had to follow her. Now, as she sits next to me, I can't help but think about how I am already corrupting this beautiful, good girl.

Driving through the streets of Savannah, I roll down the windows of my car and allow the fresh breeze to float through the interior. The wind blows Scarlette's hair all around her and my god, she is more beautiful than ever. She fights each strand, trying to tuck the loose pieces behind her ear. She lets out a laugh that sounds like a symphony to my ears.

Never have I enjoyed a moment in my life, like I am this one right now. We are carefree and wild, driving through town without a worry.

"So, where are we going?" she finally asks, once I slowdown in traffic.

"We could go to my house. My cook could make us some-thing to eat if you are hungry," I offer.

I realize once I've said it, that she may think I'm trying to get her in my bed. I mean, it wouldn't be the first time that I left school with a girl to get laid, but I've never taken them to my house before. That's too personal.

"Umm..." She shies away from me as she bites that damn lip again.

I feel my dick start to grow hard at the thought of what those sweet lips could do. Shaking my head, I try to fight that image out of my head. A girl like Scarlette deserves more respect than that. She deserves better than me, but Gabby's words have been playing on repeat in my head, and I have to see if I can do it. If I can be a good guy for Scarlette.

"If you are uncomfortable, we can go somewhere else," I state, not wanting her to feel uncomfortable.

"No, your house is fine," she says quickly.

We drive the rest of the way in silence and once I reach the gates to my house, I see her shift in her seat. Scarlette stares up at the long driveway and when she gets a view of the large, plantation home, she looks completely shocked.

"Wow, this is your house," she whispers.

"Yeah, you sound surprised," I chuckle.

She blushes and fuck me, it's adorable.

"Well, I just expected you to live somewhere more—mod-ern," she states.

Nodding, I smile up at my house. People always expect my family to live in some modern, sleek, new home in the city. Instead, my dad fell in love with this house when he was still a bachelor, and then my mom loved it, too. It's all I've ever known and I wouldn't want to live anywhere else. Well, maybe I wouldn't mind if the swaps weren't here, but that's not the point here. I love the classic feel of this house.

"A lot of people think that. I guess I'm full of surprises," I say, turning to face her again.

"That, you are," she quips.

Leaning in close, I whisper in her ear, "Were you expecting guns, men in cheap suits, and the Soprano theme song to be playing?" I ask.

I know that I am being risky playing a dangerous move with my snarky comment. I know the rumors that are spread about my family.

Scarlette's wide eyes look back at me. "No, but I did expect track suits and gold chains," she jokes.

This causes me to smile. I almost expected her to run out of my house, but instead, she made a joke, too. She is more than I ever imagined she would be.

I park the car and we get out. Walking into my house, I hear my mom in the kitchen. Scarlette grows nervous next to me.

"Ason, is that you?" mom calls out.

Her heels click against the wooden floor as she starts walking toward us. I can already feel the tension radiating off of her before she even enters the room. My mom loves me more than anything, but she also knows that I am one to fuck up and get into trouble. I hate that I worry her, but right now, I need to think of a reason for why I am not at school.

"Yeah, mom. It's me," I yell out.

As she enters the foyer, her eyes grow large as she takes in me, then Scarlette. I can tell she's confused and probably a little worried, too.

"Oh, you have a friend with you," she says, her eyes dancing between me and Scarlette.

"We left school early. They were having a pep rally for the upcoming games this weekend, but we wanted to get an early start on our tutoring," I tell her.

I can feel Scarlette staring at me. She tenses next to me as she forces a smile.

"You left to study?" mom asks, her voice rising.

I can tell that she isn't sure if she believes what I am saying or not. Since I am an expert at lying, I add more to my elaborate plan.

"Yeah, I really need to get my grades up, or I may not be able to play in the game this weekend," I explain.

It's bullshit and I worry she may figure it out. As much as I enjoy playing baseball, I don't really care if I get to play this weekend or not. Coach is always on my ass and most of my teammates only want to hang out with me to excel their own status at school.

A warm smile covers mom's face, and I almost feel bad for lying to her. "I guess it's ok then. Just don't make a habit out of skipping school." She turns to Scarlette and I grow tense. "Forgive my son and his rude manners. What's your name, dear?" mom asks Scarlette.

"Hello, Mrs. Antoni. I'm Scarlette. I am Ason's tutor," Scarlette states, her sweet smile brightening the room.

"You can call me, Willow," mom says to Scarlette.

"Well, we are going to head outside to study," I say, starting to lead Scarlette down the hallway.

"If you all need anything, just let me know. I will have the cook bring you all some food," mom yells, as I escort Scarlette out the back door.

Once we are outside, I swear I hear Scarlette exhale a breath. I lead her over to a large outdoor area equipped with a six-person dining table, fire pit, and outdoor kitchen area. Scarlette marvels at the stonework surrounding the space.

"This is beautiful," she admires.

"Thanks. My mom really enjoys entertaining out here," I tell her.

We sit down at the table and Scarlette stares blankly at me.

"I left my backpack in the car. I should go get it so we can study," she begins, going to stand.

"No, wait," I blurt out, stopping her.

Scarlette's eyes grow wide. "Oh, I thought you wanted to study," she says, nervously.

"We can, but that's not why I invited you here," I say nervously.

Scarlette's eyes narrow and then a frown appears over her face. I hate how her spark seems to die down.

"Oh. Look, I think you are nice, but if you thought I would come here and sleep with you..."

Before she can finish, I stop her. "That's not what I thought," I race out. Running a hand over my face, I realize I've already fucked this up. Maybe Gabby was wrong.

Scarlette looks defeated and I hate that I am worrying her. I've never done this before and I know that I am messing everything up.

"Then, why am I here? Why did you ask me to leave school with you?" she asks quietly.

I lean forward, moving into her personal space. She gasps and leans back in the chair. "Scarlette, I wanted to spend time with you. I don't really know what I'm doing... or how to be around you," I begin. I'm growing frustrated with myself. I want to tell her how I feel. How just the sight of her face brings me a joy that nothing else in my life ever has. I want to explain to her that knowing that I would see her every day was the only thing that got me to wake up each day and walk the halls of school.

"Ason," she says my name breathlessly, and I almost come undone.

Tucking a loose strand of hair behind her ear, I stare into her beautiful eyes. "Scarlette, I've watched you for years. Whenever you thought that no one noticed you—I did. Whenever you tried to hide from the rest of the world, I saw you shining. I know that I am not good enough for you, but I can't seem to stay away from you anymore," I confess, spilling my heart and soul to her.

She opens her mouth, but then clamps it shut again. She watches me with wide eyes and I almost feel like I'm going to explode. For a moment, I fear that I have just terrified her and she will insist that I take her home. But to my surprise, that's not at all what she says.

"I never thought you noticed me," she says so quietly, I almost don't hear her words.

How could I not notice her? While the other girls loudly flaunted their bodies and wealth, Scarlette had an unspoken beauty that called to my soul. She was everything those other girls were not. And more.

"Scarlette, I've noticed you forever. I know it's wrong for a guy like me to want you..."

"What does that mean, a guy like you? Do you think you are better than me?" she asks, her eyes starting to fill with tears.

Shaking my head, I grab her hand. She tries to pull away, my grip is strong and she can't wiggle out of my hold. Her eyes grow large as she watches me with glistening eyes.

"It's not like that at all. If anything, I think you are too good for me. Scarlette, you are sweet, smart, and beautiful. I am part of a world filled with corruption. I've never wanted to hurt you, that's why I kept my distance. However, I don't think I can do it any longer. It's so wrong for me to want you the way I do, but I can't help myself," I tell her.

I've never been vulnerable in my life. I've also never been so honest with another person before. I don't think I've ever been honest with myself, either. Scarlette brings out something in me that I just can't explain, but I want to explore it more.

"Ason, you are popular and everyone wants to have you or be you. Why would you want a girl like me? I'm nothing compared to you," she says, her head falling.

I can't stop myself. Scarlette needs to see her worth and I will ensure every day that she knows just how amazing she is. I told her the other night to stop saying she was a nobody, I guess I just had to prove to her that she was more than special. She is amazing. Placing my hand on her chin, I force her to look up. She should never hang her head. As our eyes meet, I crash my mouth against her soft lips in a kiss that ignites a raging fire in my heart and soul. She gladly accepts the kiss, slightly opening her mouth so that my tongue can explore. Her hands move to my chest and mine cup her face. Our kiss is filled with want and need and a passion so strong, it consumes my entire being.

When she finally pulls away, we are both panting and our breathing is ragged.

"I'm a selfish prick," I tell her. "I want you, but I shouldn't. You are too good for a guy like me."

"Why don't you let me make that decision," she says, breathlessly.

Those words spark a fire inside of me and I can no longer deny how I feel. "I've been watching you for years. Longing to touch you. To taste you. Always looking from afar as I kept my distance. Not ever wanting to put you in harm's way. But now that I know you, I can't stay away from you any longer," I confess. "I need you to be mine."

To my surprise and delight, Scarlette beams at me before kissing me again. I know that I should probably slow down since my mom and our staff are here at the house, but nothing can stop me from having Scarlette right now.

"I want to be yours," she speaks.

And, for the first time in my life, I feel like I can breathe.

CHAPTER 16

SCARLETTE

Ason's mom leaves to run errands and Ason and I remain at the house.

It's strange to be here alone with him, but I just can't force myself to leave either. Walking into the home of Savannah's most notorious crime family was a risky move on my part. I wasn't sure what to expect, but his mom seemed wonderful and his life feels—normal. We move inside and our kisses become more intense. I can feel the air around us shifting and my body is heated just thinking of what we can do alone in the house. Damn, I am so far gone and over my head with this guy.

"Do you want to go to my room?" he asks.

Yes.

No.

I'm torn. I want Ason, but I don't want him to think poorly of me if we have sex so early on. Though, I am not sure how much longer I can resist him.

Nodding, I smile at him, giving him permission to take my hand and lead me up the winding staircase and toward his bedroom.

When we enter his room, I stand for a moment and take in the surroundings. The walls are painted a navy blue and the room is accented with white, red, and tan paintings and sheets on his large, four-poster bed.

Ason walks us over to the bed and we both sit on the edge of the mattress.

"We don't have to do anything that you aren't comfortable with," he says, looking longingly into my eyes.

I know he is offering me an out, but I am not sure that I want an out. I've never felt such a strong need to do something so wrong in all of my life. Honestly, I wasn't even sure what I would be comfortable with, but I trusted Ason— as crazy as that seems, and wanted to have my first experiences be with him.

Leaning in, I surprise us both when I crash my lips to his. In seconds, we are kissing and tearing at one another's clothes. All logical thoughts and reservations are long gone. All I can think about is being with Ason. He may destroy me later, but I can't worry about that now. Reckless and untamed is the only way I can describe myself right now, but I am too far gone to stop now.

Ason crawls on top of me, pulling his shift off in the process. Instinctively, my hands slide over his abs and I feel my panties soaking. He smiles wickedly at me as he tugs at my shift, lifting it over my head and tossing it somewhere on the floor. He's staring at me with such intensity, it causes my breath to catch in my throat. I've never been this exposed to anyone before, but with Ason, it almost feels right.

"You are so beautiful," he says, trailing kisses down my neck and to my breasts.

He massages one breast as his other hand begins sliding up my skirt. When his fingers touch my soaked panties, he stops kissing me and smiles. "Damn, you are so wet," he growls out.

My face flushes and I feel so embarrassed. "I'm sorry," I mutter out.

"No, this is so fucking hot," he says, taking my nipple in his mouth and sucking and biting.

The feeling is euphoric and my hands begin teasing his hair as I begin craving more and more of him. His dick grows hard and rubs against my thigh. Without thinking, I begin fumbling with his zipper on his pants. He helps me by sliding them down his legs and his dick springs out of his boxer shorts.

As one of his finger's dips inside of me, I let out a moan and throw my head back in delight.

"This feels so good," I gasp, as he begins pumping in and out of me.

"Has anyone ever touched you before?" he asks me.

"No," I say.

He smiles and I know that was the answer he wanted. Ason is animalistic and for some reason, I can tell that he likes that I am untouched and unexplored.

"Have you ever been fucked?" he asked.

His crass question should cause me to stop this and run away. But, it doesn't. Instead, he has me wanting to beg him to be my first. As though I am having some exciting out of body experience, I am loving this new person that is slowly emerging from me. I don't know who she is, but I am ready to get to know her.

"No, never," I say, staring into his eyes.

This ignites Ason and he goes back to kissing and fingering me until I feel like I am going to explode. Just when I feel myself reaching my breaking point, he stops and leans over to his bed side table. Opening a drawer, he pulls out a condom. It bothers me for a second that he has them ready and available, but I have to remind myself that Ason is a known party body who girls throw themselves at. Maybe that should have made me stop this behavior, but it didn't. I just pushed that thought aside as I watched him roll the condom over his dick. Licking my lips, I found myself hungry for him.

As I watch him hoover above me, my chest heaves at the anticipation of what is about to come. He slowly slides inside of me and I arch my back, welcoming him. As I stretch to fit all of him, it hurts briefly, but then that pain morphs into an indescribable pleasure. He begins rocking into me, slow and steady at first. When I raise my hips up and call out his name, he begins moving faster and going harder.

His mouth covers my moans and all I can do is allow myself to give in to this moment. Grabbing my hips, he flips me over and pulls my ass up to him. I steady myself on my hands and my mouth falls wide open when he begins pounding into me from behind. I've never been so turned on and pleasured in all my life. My first time having sex is wild and incredible and I ride out this high for as long as I possibly can.

I hear Ason begin to grunt from behind me and he pumps one more time before we both reach our climax and come together. Falling beside me, he pants as his chest rises and falls rapidly. Lying next to him, I watch him in awe. Even if he pushes me away tomorrow, this moment will forever remain in my mind.

"Are you ok?" he asks, once he catches his breath.

"Yes, that was...incredible," I say, smiling over at him.

"Did I hurt you?" he asks.

I hate that he asks me that. Knowing I was a virgin makes me feel a little less than compared to him.

"No, it felt great," I tell him.

Pulling the sheets up to my chest, I have no idea what to do next. When Ason grabs my hand and holds it, I feel my heart swell. Did this mean as much to him as it did for me? For the sake of my heart, I hope so.

Nodding, he turns his head to face me. "I'm glad. I can't tell you how long I've dreamed of doing that," he admits. "I'm just glad I got to be your first."

His words leave me momentarily speechless. I still don't understand his infatuation with me, but I am enjoying it.

Squeezing his hand, I turn and smile back at him. "I'm glad you were my first, too. I still don't understand this," I say, glancing between us.

"We don't have to understand it right now. Just know, I don't want anyone else touching you," he says with such intensity, it startles me.

"Ok," I whisper, still stunned.

We lay there for a while longer before I realize we have to get back to school so I can get my car. The last thing I want to do is leave my bed, but I know that I need to go. Plus, I don't want his mom or dad to come home and find us in bed. That isn't the impression I want to make on them. Even though being in the mafia, I'm sure they have seen far worse...

"I need to get back to my car," I say, hating to ruin this moment.

There is a calmness about the moment as we lay together, tangled in one another. It's the most comfortable I have ever felt and that is a strange thought.

"I really don't want to leave," Asons says, sitting up and placing a kiss to my shoulder.

Warmth spreads through me and if I don't get up now, I never will.

"Me either," I admit.

"I want to see you again. Soon," he demands.

Normally, someone telling me what to do would bother me, but with Ason, I find it strangely endearing.

"You will," I say, sitting up and meeting him eye-to-eye.

We get out of bed and dress in silence. Ason moves to his bathroom and allows me a moment of privacy, even though he just saw every inch of my exposed body. Once we are dressed, he kisses me one last time and my knees almost go weak. I am not sure I will ever come down from the ecstasy I am on right now.

Ason held my hand as he drove me back to the school parking lot.

It was a surreal feeling sitting in his car, holding his hand, after making out with him all afternoon. We somehow managed to get some of his studying completed, and his mom was super sweet. She pretended not to spy on us, but we knew she was there. Never in my life had I felt so happy as I did now. I kept waiting for the bubble to pop and Ason to tell me this was all some cruel joke. But as he smiled at me, I felt his emotions for me radiating off of him. He was different from the guy I had seen throughout the years. He wasn't the arrogant Elite who walked the halls as though he owned them. No, he was kind and sweet and unsure of himself. He was like me in ways I never thought possible.

When we reached the school, Ason pulled up next to my vehicle. We both sat still for a moment. I didn't want to leave his car. I felt like once I did, I would wake up from my dream.

Leaning across the seat, Ason kissed me. "I will call you later?" he says.

"Ok," I said, smiling back at him.

When I got in my car, I watched him pull away before I drove off. As I made my way home, I couldn't stop smiling like an idiot. My phone rang and Macy's name appeared over the display in my car.

"Hello," I answered, sounding way too happy.

"Where did you go?" she asked.

I could hear people in the background talking and laughing.

"I decided to leave," I said. "Where are you?"

"I'm leaving Dodds Bakery. A bunch of us came here after the pep rally," she said. The background noise disappeared and I heard her start her car. She was alone now.

"I need to tell you something, but you have to swear not to say anything or judge me," I began.

My stomach churned as I went to tell her my secret. I wasn't even sure if she would believe me.

"Ok. You are freaking me out," she chuckled.

Sighing, I gripped the steering wheel as I began. "I left school today with Ason Antoni." I stopped talking, waiting to hear her reply.

A loud screech erupted and I almost jumped out of my seat. "Ason Antoni! Are you serious right now?"

"Yeah. I was going to hide out in the library, but he found me. We went back to his house to study..." I said, but Macy's voice cut me off.

"You went to his house? Scarlette, I feel like I am talking to an entirely different person. What is going on?" she cried out.

"I honestly have no idea. Ason is different from what I thought. He kissed me," I stated.

"Ok, stop talking. Are you home?" Macy rushed out.

"I'm almost home. Five minutes away."

"I will be there in two minutes," she yelled, then ended the call.

I laughed as I drove the rest of the way home.

"Ok, tell me everything," Macy said, holding onto one of my decorative pillows as she sat on my bed.

I lay next to her, staring up at the ceiling as I struggled to collect my thoughts. There was so much to tell her and I didn't even know what to say. As the words spilled out, Macy listened intently. Her smile grew wider as I talked and I could feel my cheeks blushing.

"This is beyond amazing," Macy said. "You and Ason are dating. He popped your little virgin cherry!"

Shaking my head, I held up my hand to stop her. "We aren't dating. We are..." Honestly, I had no idea what we were. "We are just figuring things out."

"Scarlette, you have left me speechless. I am so proud of you. I never thought that you would skip school, but to hear that you and Ason Antoni hooked up...I am just in awe of you," she laughed.

"Don't be in awe of me," I started. While I felt like I was floating on cloud nine, nothing had truly been confirmed yet. Once we got to school, in public, the truth would finally come out. "We will see how Ason reacts at school on Monday."

"Maybe he truly likes you. I mean, Scarlette you are hot. You don't see it, but you really are," Macy told me.

I blushed. I never thought of myself as anything special, but maybe being with Ason made me special.

"He was the first person who ever made me feel cool for not being cool. Like not fitting in, somehow made me special in his eyes." The words spilled out of my mouth before I could stop me.

"Scarlette, you don't see yourself the way the rest of us do. This may be your opportunity to finally shine," Macy said.

We spent the next few hours talking. When my parents finally got home, Macy left and begged me to call her if I heard from Ason again. After a dinner which consisted of listening to my parents go on and on about their trip, I retired to my bedroom to get some homework completed. It was almost as though the afternoon had never happened. I had been swept away by the most sought-after boy at school and then brought back to my house where I was once again, the quiet, lonely girl that no one really knew. Honestly, I was like a twisted version of Cinderella. Minus the evil stepsisters.

By ten that night, I had given up hope that I would hear from Ason.

Yawning, I packed away my school books and changed into a pair of silky red pajama shorts and a tank top. My heart hurt a little at the thought that maybe he had played me. I didn't want to harp on it, though. If I did, it may drive me crazy. Crawling into bed, I closed my eyes and was almost asleep when I heard my phone ringing from my bed side stand. Glancing at the screen, I see Ason's name appear.

I almost laugh as I remember the night he brought me home, drunk off my ass, and programmed his number into my phone. Answering, I wait for that deep voice that sends chills down my spine.

"Hey," he says, sounding tired.

"Hi," I reply.

I stare up at the ceiling, watching as the shadows from the window dance above me. The glow of the silver moon illuminates the world outside and it's almost magical to look at.

"What are you doing?" he asks, nonchalantly.

"Well, I was getting ready to go to bed," I tell him. "You know, it's pretty late."

Ason chuckles and the sound makes me smile. "I didn't realize you had a bed time," he jokes.

Even though his slight is meant in fun, it reminds me of just how different we really are. I'm the girl who goes to bed early because I don't have plans. It's a Friday night and I'm tucked away in bed. Ason is probably out at some wild party and laughing at how lame I am.

"When you don't have any other plans..." my words trail off. Closing my eyes, I internally cringe at how dumb I sound. Why do I have word vomit right now? Can't I think of anything sexy or clever to say?

Nope, definitely not.

"How about we change that?" Ason says, a slight rise in his voice.

"What are you talking about?" I ask, sitting up in bed.

"Go to your window," he huffs out.

Before I know what I am doing, I throw the blankets off my body and jump out of bed. Padding over to my window, I glance out into the dark night. Suddenly, a figure moves out of the shadows and stands near a light shining from the house.

Ason.

My heart quickens at the sight of him. Tall, dark, and brooding, he stands under the yellow light, a wicked smile covering his perfectly chiseled face. I swear, he looks like he was hand made by the Gods for humans to admire. What in the hell is he doing here?

"What are you doing here?" I hiss out.

I try not to squeal. What would my parents think if they knew there was a boy outside of my bedroom window. And, not just any boy.

Ason Antoni.

The son of a Savannah mob boss.

The Elite.

They probably wouldn't even believe it, even if they saw it for themselves.

"I came here to see you. Come outside," Ason states.

It's not a question or an offer. No, this is a demand.

Just like earlier today, when he offered to take me out of school, it wasn't really a question. He was making a demand and I didn't even bat an eye. With Ason, he has this hold over me that makes me forget all senses and right and wrong blend together.

"This is insane, Ason. It's late at night," I try to argue, but I think we both know it's of no use.

"I will be waiting in my car," Ason says, and then hangs up the phone.

I watch as he turns and his figure slowly fades into the darkness once again.

Chapter 17

Scarlette

Sometimes in life, you have to just jump off the ledge.

Forget all rational thought.

Forget your own fears and trepidations.

Forget how wrong something may be, and just focus on how right it feels in the moment.

I'm being wild and reckless as I tip-toe down my stairs and then holding my breath, open the back door to my house. Slipping out into the cool, night air I race across the yard until I reach the street. I've never snuck out of my house before and until today, I had never skipped school, either. Ason's car is parked only a few feet away and as I approach, my body tingles with excitement.

"Hey," a voice hisses to my right.

I stop moving, almost stumbling over my own two feet at the sound.

Ason is standing against his sleek car, arms crossed over his massive chest, and a Cheshire smile lighting the darkness around him.

Folding my arms across my chest, I stare back at him. "You are crazy, you know that, right?" I ask, a slight laughter to my voice.

Reaching out, Ason pulls me forward and I fall against his chest. We are so close now that I can feel his warm breath against my cheek. "I'm pretty crazy about you," he breathes.

At any other moment, I would have found that line completely ridiculous and made fun of it, but with Ason, there's something so genuine about him, that all I can do is melt.

"That's pretty cheesy," I smirk.

Ason lets his head fall back as he laughs. There's a light in his eyes tonight that makes him look almost happy.

"So, what are you really doing here?" I ask, my hands still on his rock-hard chest. His heart beats under my fingers and I internally count the beats.

"Honestly, I don't know. I just really wanted to see you. Sorry it's so late, I had a family dinner that I couldn't miss," he says, though there is a hint of frustration ringing in his voice.

I've noticed that his family is a touchy subject. I wonder what is going on there, but I don't dare spoil this moment and ask.

"Shouldn't you be at some party?" I ask.

I don't know why I'm pushing. Why I am struggling to believe that he's really here. We had sex earlier, but this is hard to believe?

Shaking his head, Ason's intense gaze renders me helpless. "There is nowhere else I would rather be right now, then right here," he says, snaking his arm around my waist and puling me in for a kiss. "With you. I need you again."

We start out slow and sweet, but then as the kiss deepens, we move to needy and desire fueled. My hands go to his hair and his remain locked on my waist. He's holding me so tightly, as though he fears I may slip away. His tongue parts my lips and I gladly accept the intrusion. My body heats to inferno levels and I swear, I hope this moment never ends. I have no idea what I'm doing, but for the first time in my life, I am throwing caution to the wind and just enjoying the moment. We slip into the back seat of his car and he fucks me two more times that night.

By Monday morning, I was in an Ason filled haze.

We spent most of Sunday texting one another and I couldn't get our late-night rendezvous out of my head. Now, as I walk into school, I feel a different mood in the atmosphere. I walk down the halls with a slight smile on my face. Maybe it's the fact that I have a secret that no one knows, or that for the first time in my life I feel happy and content. Either way, I feel like a new person.

"Wow, someone is in a good mood!" Macy says, as she sidles up next to me.

We walk over to the coffee cart stationed outside of the front office. It still seems crazy to me that we have such luxuries at our school.

I pretend to study the menu, even though I know it by heart. "What? I can't have a good day?" I ask.

Shaking her head, Macy narrows her eyes at me. "I wonder if it has anything to do with a certain boy," she teases. Her eyes sparkle with delight knowing my secret.

"Shhh," I reprimand her. "I have no idea what we are, so I don't want to say anything about it. I just feel different today," I explain.

"Well, I think it's great either way. You deserve to be happy," she tells me.

We both order French vanilla Capuchinos and then make our way to our lockers. Allowing the caffeine and sugar to blend with my own euphoria only causes my mood to become more cheerful. I gather my things at my locker and then as I turn to head toward my homeroom, Macy stops me and glances around before lowering her voice.

"Are you going to the baseball game tonight?" she asks quietly.

I honestly hadn't thought about it. In my years at Royal Elite Academy, I had never been to any of our sporting events. It just never seemed to interest me. At least, not until now.

"I don't know," I say biting my lip.

"You should totally go. He may appreciate you being there," she says, winking before she walks away.

I'm left standing in the middle of the hallway, wondering if I should actually consider going. Just as I gain my senses back, my world shifts as The Elites turn down the hallway. Gabby and Ason lead the way as Micah and Talon fall in behind them. Everyone stops and stares, moving out of their way as they part the hallway like the red sea. My heart rate picks up and all I can do is walk faster as I rush to get my class. This thing between me and Ason makes me giddy as hell, but it also confuses me. I have no idea if I am allowed to smile at him or even talk to him. Will he ignore me? Will he get angry if I approach him at school?

I allow those thoughts to consume me the rest of the day.

After school, I head to the library to check my tutoring schedule this week. Since Ason has a game today, our session has been moved to Wednesday. As I'm leaving the library, I feel a hand reach out and grab me.

Spinning, I lock eyes with Ason.

"Why have you avoided me today?" he asks, not bothering to say hello.

I stare back at him and for a moment, I am not sure what to say. How do you tell a boy who you are insanely crushing on, that you aren't sure if you are supposed to talk to him in public?

"I wasn't sure if it was ok for me to say anything," I tell him. Biting my lip, I feel my old self return as that awkward tension fills me.

Ason moves toward me, closing in on me. His thumb lands on my bottom lip, tracing over my lip, and I'm stunned speechless.

"That drives me crazy," he growls out.

"What does?" I ask, my voice barely above a whisper.

"When you bite your lip like that," he states. "You didn't think you could talk to me?" he asks, almost as though this insight is confusing to him. He also barely touches the surface of his comment about me biting my lip.

Doesn't Ason understand the power he holds over everyone here at the Royal Elite Academy? He and the rest of his crew are not approachable by any means.

I look down at my feet then back up to his heated gaze. "Ason, we have been over this. I'm a nobody here and you are...a God," I say, as my cheeks blush from the admission.

His thumb moves down my chin and then he slides his fingers over my neck. My skin tingles from his touch and my breathing becomes ragged. He's being reckless right now and I secretly love it. I've had crushes on boys before, but never have I felt this aroused. I've always been too shy or self-conscious to ever talk to guys I've liked. But now. I'm standing in the middle of the hallway as freaking Ason Antoni touches me like a complete savage.

"Scarlette, and I've already told you that to me, you aren't a nobody. You are so beautiful," he breathes, his fingers moving toward my breasts.

I let out a slight gasp as I wait for him to move further down, but just as I feel like I can't take his teasing anymore, he moves his hands over to my arms. My heart falls a little, but I'm also relieved, too. I have no idea how far he would have gone, or how far I would have allowed him to go.

"Come to my game tonight," he says.

"What will people think?" I rush out.

Ason shrugs. "Why do you care what people think?"

This is a question I have pondered over myself for years. No one notices me, so why do I care what people think? Other than Macy, I don't have relationships with other people. I think being left alone so much as caused this hard shell to grow over my skin. At some point, I accepted the fact that I'm just not that important to people.

"I know that I shouldn't but I just worry..." My words trail off, as I really don't know what to say.

To someone like Ason, my dilemma doesn't make sense. Don't get me wrong; I've always wished that I could be one of those girls who had loads of self-confidence and had a group of friends surrounding her. But, that just wasn't in the cards for me. I made this life of solitude for myself.

"I have to go to the locker room to meet the team. I will see you at the game," he states, leaning in and placing a kiss on my mouth.

As quickly as he showed up, he's gone and I am left once again hopelessly lost under Ason's spell.

Chapter 18

Ason

The crowd cheers as we score another run.

The bright lights over the field seems to magnify the space before me. I stand in the dugout, watching as another one of my teammates rounds second and is called safe on third base. I'm up next in the lineup, but all I can focus on right now is Scarlette.

Earlier, I had told her to come to my game. It wasn't a question, but a command. It was something I had inherited from my father; the need to control situations. I wanted Scarlette—needed her, and I wasn't going to take no, for an answer. The fact that she hadn't been touched by any other guy turned me on even more. Keeping tabs on her over the years, I had sadistically enjoyed watching her steer away from guys who I knew wanted to date her. She never saw her own worth, but that was paying off for me now. I know it makes me sound like a sick bastard, and maybe I truly am, but I can't help myself. When it comes to Scarlette, there isn't anything I wouldn't do to make her mine.

My eyes scan the crowd until I spot Scarlette at the back of the bleachers. She's with her friend, Macy, and I can't help but notice that Scarlette seems uncomfortable. While the rest of the crowd cheers and talks about the game, she sits quietly next to her friend.

"Ason, you're up on deck," coach shouts.

I grab my helmet and bat and make my way out of the dugout. When it's my turn to hit, I head to the plate, but before I ready myself, I catch Scarlette's eyes and smile. People in the stands notice my admiring her and their heads all turn as they search for who has my attention. I can already hear their whispers and see their shocked faces when they realize it's Scarlette that I am smiling at.

As Scarlette realizes that it's not just me looking at her, I can see her blush heating her face from here on the field. I can see that she is fighting whether to smile or be angry. I turn my attention back to the game and when the ball comes flying at me at over fifty miles per hour, I swing with all my strength and hear as the crack of the bat pings in the air. Without thinking, I drop the bat and begin racing toward first base. The crowd roars to life as they cheer me on. My teammates are hyped up, banging on the dugout walls as I touch first base and sprint toward second. When I slide into third, I stand up smiling as I'm called safe. Instead of looking back to my team, I look to Scarlette who is standing and clapping, too. Seeing her cheering for me is the best high I could ever experience. She's the only one I care about right now. By tomorrow, the entire world is going to know that Scarlette is mine.

CHAPTER 19

SCARLETTE

My cheeks burn with a raging fire.

Partly from the embarrassment from the stares I received all evening and the other part from smiling and cheering for Ason. After winning ten to fourteen, the team raced off the field. Pulling Macy to the parking lot, I ignored her complaints as we left before the partying began.

After Ason smiled up at me during the game, a few people had tried to ask me what was going on between me and Ason. Of course, I had no idea what to say. A few girls were even giving me evil glares and Tara, the girl from the video and one of the school's cheerleaders, glared at me all throughout the game.

"I don't understand why you didn't want to stay," Macy said, pouting next to me as I drove out of the school parking lot.

The lights from the field faded behind us as I drove away. Our prestigious academy had college level sports complexes. It seemed a little over the top, but I guess that's what you get from a school that caters to Savannah's elite.

"Didn't you see how people were looking at me?" I asked her, trying to keep my focus on the road.

Macy's face lit up like a Christmas tree. "Hell yeah, I saw how everyone was looking at you. Scarlette, I've been getting texts all night. People are asking who you are, how you know

Ason, and what is going on between the two of you," she says, showing me her phone.

I shake my head, refusing to let this mania get to me. Inside, I'm nervous as to what this all means.

After I drop Macy off at her house, I drive home with a bundle of nerves filling my stomach. My parents are home for once and when I walk into the kitchen, they greet me.

"Scarlette, we were surprised that you weren't home," my dad says, offering a hug.

"I went to a baseball game," I tell them.

My mom, who was busy wiping down the kitchen counter, stops and smiles brightly at me. "Really? That's a nice change," she states.

"It was fun," I say.

I talk to them a few more minutes before finally heading up to my bedroom. The last thing I want to do is try and explain me and Ason to my parents. I barely understand it myself.

After showering and changing into a pair of pajamas, I crawl into bed with a mystery novel from one of my favorite authors.

I see my phone lighting up as a call begins to come through. It's Ason.

"Hello," I answer.

"Where did you go?" he rushes out.

I can hear people talking in the background.

"Oh, I had to get home," I lie.

"I wanted to celebrate our win with you," Ason states, and my heart aches.

I feel bad for leaving without saying anything to him. I was just too nervous to stay any longer. I had to get out of the stadium before the crowd had a chance to ask me any other questions.

"I'm sorry I left before I could say congratulations. I hope you enjoy the party," I say, cringing a little on the inside.

"If you aren't coming, then I am not going to the party," Ason growls out.

I shoot up in bed. Ason is so crazy.

"What?"

"I'm leaving the stadium now. I'm coming to your house. Get dressed," he states, and then the phone goes dead.

I hold the device in my hand, trying to figure out what just happened. Ason infuriates me, but I can't help but fall to his embrace.

I jump out of bed and quickly pull on a pair of jeans and a long sleeve black shirt. When I return downstairs, my parents are watching a movie in the living room. They both look surprised to see me dressed again.

"Is something wrong?" mom asks.

I almost chuckle at her reaction. They think something is the matter since I am dressed and about to go out like a normal teenager.

"Well, a friend called and wants to go hangout for a little while," I tell them, fidgeting with my phone in my hands.

They glance at one another. Clearly, they don't know how to handle this. It's a school night, but I've never asked to go out before. I can see them torn.

"I guess that's ok, but don't stay gone too long," mom says, smiling.

"Thanks!" I yell, as I run to the front door.

I want to meet Ason on the driveway. I would die if he came to the door and my parents were to meet him. Eventually, I'm sure I will have to explain him to them, but I need to prepare myself for that. Telling my parents that I'm going out with an Antoni will be...interesting.

I see the headlights of Ason's car heading toward me and my heart begins to race. When he pulls into my driveway, I open the passenger door and the smile on Ason's face causes my heart to flutter. His scent assaults me and I internally memorize it.

"You are very bossy, you know," I say, as I slide into the cool leather seat.

"No, I just am very assertive," he says, grinning from ear-to-ear.

I giggle at this as we back out my driveway. "So, where are we going?" I ask, watching as the houses blur by.

"It's a surprise," he says, winking at me.

My heart flutters but a ball of nervous energy flows through me. What if he wants to take me to a party? Biting my lip, I begin to fidget with my phone as I contemplate what to say next. I have questions for him, but I am also enjoying the silence between us. As we drive, there is this comfortable vibe floating between us. It's nice.

"Ok. So, why aren't you hanging out with your friends?" I dare to ask him.

I see Ason's jaw tense and he drives a little faster, which causes my nervousness to only intensify.

"I was with them earlier, but I needed to see you," he said, as though it were an admission that he was afraid to make. "Talon, Micah, and Gabby are at a party with the rest of the school."

He frowns and I hate seeing him look so sad. "What's wrong?" I ask quietly.

The lights from a passing car streak across his face and illuminates his face. I am struck breathless by his handsomeness. Without warning, he reaches across the car and grabs my hand, squeezing tightly. He shakes his head and for a moment, I don't think he is going to tell me what is ailing him. But when he finally speaks, I am listening intently. Hanging on his every word.

His words are tense. "I've spent my entire life surrounded by my friends. We are practically family; in fact, I think of them as family more than anything. But, there are things I hide from them that I just can't seem to hide from you," he says, daring a look my way.

His gaze heats me to my core and I force myself to look out the window in the hopes that I don't catch ablaze. I notice that we have driven down to the riverfront. I sit up a little straighter as I notice our new location. I don't dare speak as he pulls into a parking spot facing the riverfront.

As the car turns off, we sit in the darkness and silence for what feels like forever. "Scarlette, you know that I am an Antoni..." he says, a worried expression lacing his features.

"Yes," I say, nodding.

He's still holding my hand and I squeeze back, giving him the comfort that I feel that he needs.

We both stare out over the water, as a large boat sails past us. It's quiet here in the night. It's nice and I see why he brought me here.

"There are things in my life that are just out of my control," he sighs, and runs a hand through his hair. "My future has been planned out for me, even before I was born. Gabby, Micah, and Talon have all embraced the lives that we live, but it's not what I want," he states flatly. I know that he is referring to the mafia, but I don't dare say it aloud. With the mafia in Savannah, it's something that you know exists, but you never speak of. Sort of like a secret society. Instead, I listen. Ason seems like he needs to say this; to get these emotions off his chest. As he continues, I watch his face carefully. "I want something different. I want more than the life my father has created. I can't tell him that, it would destroy him."

I feel his pain and I want nothing more than to take it all away for him. My pulse is racing as I stare at him. I need to say something now.

"Sometimes, I wish that my life was different, too," I explain.

I know that my life and struggles can't compare to what Ason is going through, but it's all I have to offer right now.

His eyes seem to lighten and he doesn't look as severe as it did just moments before.

"How is it that you seem to find a way to calm me down?" he asks, his voice filled with confusion. Shaking his head, he offers a sad smile. "When I was a little kid, my parents sent me to a therapist for my outbursts," he said, using hand quotes at the word, outbursts. "I've seen men killed. I've heard stories from my father and uncles; about the brutal ways they have tortured men. How they have lied and cheated the system to get the power and money they have today. I love my parents, I truly do. I even had mad respect for my dad, but the life he created isn't the one I want and I fear that if I don't say something soon, my own turmoil may kill me."

His chest rises and falls again as his anger springs to life once again. I can't imagine how difficult it would be to have such a conflict hanging over your head each and every day. I squeeze is hand and do my best to try and calm him down again.

Sighing, I open my mouth and hope that what comes out, will settle Ason's soul. "I'm glad that I can help you feel calm. I won't pretend to understand your life, but I can be here to listen to you when you need to talk."

Ason stared blankly at me as if I am a puzzle he is trying to figure out. "You know that by being with me, you are putting yourself in danger, right?" he asks, a slight hint of anger in his tone.

I'm not sure what to think of that. I'm not blind or naïve. Everyone in Savannah knows who the Antoni's are. We know the stories and the business dealings that everyday people know to steer clear from. Still though, none of that scares me away from the feelings I have for Ason. Being here with him, having my heart yearn for him, is so unlike me—but it feels so right.

"Are you telling me that to push me away, or to just remind us both?" I ask.

"As much as I know that I should push you away, I can't. Having you in my life is the only good thing I have right now. I just worry about you..." his words trail off.

Leaning over, I kiss him hard. Putting all of my feelings for him into the moment. At first, Ason is startled, but as he starts fisting my hair, he deepens the kiss. We are nothing more than hands and moans as we can't stop this road we are journeying down. His hand slips down to my waist and as I push harder against him, he moves me so that I am now straddling his lap. I can feel him growing hard beneath me and that sparks something wild inside of me that I have never felt before. I start grinding on him and when he moans, that gives me more motivation and courage to let out the freaky side of me that I have apparently been hiding. My core clenches and tingles as I dry hump him. His finger slips into my pants and an electric current flows through me. Anxious energy fills me as I silently beg for him to move his finger further down. When his finger begins rubbing my clit, I let my head fall back as our kiss breaks. His lips quickly move to my neck and down to my breasts as one finger slips inside of me. I can't help my own moan as I allow him to finger me while kissing all over my body. As my body begins to reach my climax, Ason can feel it, too, and he begins pumping his fingers deeper and harder inside of me until I reach the wave of ecstasy I have been waiting for. Now, it's my turn to make him come. Unzipping his pants, I take his full length and begin sucking him into my mouth. It doesn't take long before he is calling out my name and I am swallowing every ounce of his come.

I fall back against his steering wheel and it's only then that I realize we just had another intimate moment in a car, in a public parking lot. Realization strikes me like a lightning bolt and I scramble to get off of his lap.

"What's wrong?" Ason asks, as he adjusts himself.

"We just...what if someone saw..." I ramble on, my cheeks burning with fire at the embarrassment boiling to the surface.

A chuckle rumbles from his chest and Ason pulls me back toward him. "The windows are tinted and there isn't anyone else out here," he says, pointing to the car windows.

He's right; the windows are dark and we seem to be isolated in the parking lot. Still, I can't believe I lost all control like that. I've never been that girl, but hot damn, if it didn't feel amazing. Ason says that when he's with me, I make him feel better. But when I'm with Ason, I feel like I can finally be the me that has been hiding beneath layers of sadness.

"I've never done something like that before," I say, nervous of my admission.

"Good. You will only do that with me?" he says, cocking his head to the side.

All I can do is shake my head, yes.

"I love that," he growls out.

"What?" I ask, thinking I heard him wrong.

"I love that no other guy has touched you. That no one else has tasted you. I'm your first and last," he says.

With Ason, everything he says is a command. Not a question. But a demand. Why do I feel myself smiling at the thought of this? Why does knowing that Ason wants me make me so giddy inside?

I love this new side of me and I fear that I may be falling in love with Ason, too.

CHAPTER 20

ASON

Slipping my finger in my mouth, I sucked Scarlette's juices. She tasted sweet and delicious. Now that I had had a taste of her, I knew I would never be able to get enough of her. Pulling back into my driveway, I spotted Micah's large truck. Great, what the fuck was he doing here?

Heading inside my house, it was relatively quiet. As I made my way upstairs, I could hear the sounds of Call of Duty playing on my X-box in my bedroom. Walking inside, Micah and Talon were sitting on my floor, their controllers in their hands as they played a game on my large television. It's not unusual for them to be in my room. Hell, it would be weird if they weren't always at my house. We are family—brothers and right now, they are getting on my last nerves just like pesky brothers.

"What the hell are you guys doing here?" I ask, as I kick off my boots.

I think about heading to the bathroom to rub one out because Scarlette was like a drug to me. Even though I had her earlier, I found myself wanting her again.

Micah turns to look at me, but Talon never takes his eyes off of the game.

"I think we should be the one asking questions," Micah says slyly.

"Why did you bail from the party? Everyone wanted to see you," Talon chimes in.

I fall onto my bed, watching the game. "Why does it matter? Did you all get laid tonight?" I ask, already knowing the answer.

"Hell yeah, we did," Micah shouts.

Ignoring the comment, I scroll through my phone and see several missed calls and texts. "Where's Gabby?" I ask.

Shrugging, Talon turns to look at me finally. "No clue. She said she had something to do after we all left the party."

I wondered what she was doing. I didn't have any missed texts from her and that was strange, but right now, I needed to worry about getting rid of Talon and Micah so I could jerk off and then go to bed.

Talon kills Micah in the game and they both throw their controllers down. As they turn to face me, I drop my phone on the bed and glare back at them.

"Alright, what is it?" I ask them.

"Have you given any thought to what you want to do?" Micah asks me.

I know that they mean well and that they are only bugging me about my decision because I'm the oldest and they already view me as their leader, but what they don't realize is that this isn't easy for me.

Releasing a sigh, I know that I can't continue to be an asshole to them when they ask. They deserve an answer. "I know that whatever role I take, I want to ensure that I can have a normal life, too," I begin. "Guys, we have lived the mafia lifestyle since we were born. Don't you guys ever think about having a regular job?" I ask.

As soon as the words exit my mouth, I instantly regret them. Micah's eyes almost bug out of his head and Talon looks at me like he didn't just hear what I said. The backlash I am going to receive will be hell for sure.

Jumping to his feet, Micah throws his hands up in the air. "Don't give me this wanting a regular job bullshit, Ason," he yells. "We are in the mafia. We live it, breathe it, and fucking own this shit. No one gets out of this life." His eyes are intense as he stares back at me.

I move off the bed, taking slow and easy steps toward him. Micah has a temper and he has swung on me before. Talon jumps between us, raising his hands up to separate us.

"I don't want out. I just want a different role," I plead.

It's Talon who turns this time and yells. "Different role? Ason, you are going to be the boss. Our capo. How could you even consider not taking that role?"

Shaking my head, I move to my window and stare out over the vast landscape. It's eerie to look at in the quiet of the night. As I turn back to face them, they are awaiting my response. "I will be your Capo, but things will be different."

This seems to ease their worries a little. Micah's shoulders relax and Talon's breathing goes back to normal.

"Ason, we are family. Just tell us, what are you so afraid of?" Talon asks.

Their anger is gone, but in its place is concern. I'm not sure I prefer the second one. I can tell them the truth; that I don't want to be a killer. That as a child, hearing the gun shots ring out from the swamps behind the house, would elicit such horrific nightmares in me, that I couldn't sleep. I became an angry child and that same anger followed me into my teenage years. Listening to the stories of my father and uncle would flash wicked images into my mind that I could never escape from. They thought they were training me to be a man. To one day be the leader of the Antoni Mafia Family, but all they did was instill a terror inside of me that plagued me. Do I want to be the boss? Sure. Do I want to kill people? No. While I always understood that my father only hurt those who hurt others, it was the physical act of killing that scarred me. I envied my dad. Looked up to him as a strong and powerful man. But there was a side of him that enjoyed the vicious and cruel murders. He found pleasure in their pain and their deaths brought him peace.

"I'm not afraid of anything. I just... have someone that I care about now. Her safety is important to me," I admit.

While using Scarlette as a scapegoat isn't right, it is partially true. I do worry about Scarlette. Her safety means the world to me and I would die if anything happened to her.

Micah smiles and smacks Talon on his back.

"This is about a girl? Who is it?" Micah says, with a smirk.

"Is it that crazy cheerleader, Tara? Damn, we all saw that video where she was all over you at the party a couple of weekends ago," Talon adds in.

"What? No. There is a video?" My mind is reeling right now. "No, her name is Scarlette. She was my tutor. Only Gabby knows," I tell them.

Saying her name aloud feels good. I can't help the smile that crosses my face.

"Oh shit, Ason is smiling," Micah taunts me.

"Shut up," I yell.

They both start hysterically laughing and I want to beat them both senseless. A sudden knock on my bedroom door startles me, but Micah and Talon don't seem to be bothered at all.

When my mom walks in, I sigh.

"Hey, boys. I heard yelling," she states.

My mom is beautiful and one of the kindest people I know. If she can be happy living in the mafia, maybe Scarlette can, too. Oh shit, I have it bad for this girl.

"Yeah, Ason is acting all pissy because he likes a girl," Micah laughs.

A bright smile beams across my mom's face. She leans against the door frame and laughs. "A girl, huh? Is it that pretty girl you brought over the other day? The one with long, brown hair?" mom asks.

All I can do is nod. This is the last thing I want to talk to my mom about right now. Especially, with dumb and dumber here.

"She was at our house?" Micah asks, his jaw falling to the floor.

"Damn, this must be serious," Talon whistles.

I go to run at them both, but my mom shouts. "Enough, boys. I'm going back to bed. Keep your nonsense down," she says, smiling as she closes my bedroom door.

For the rest of the night, Talon and Micah do their best to make fun of me as we take out our aggression in Call of Duty.

CHAPTER 21

SCARLETTE

By Monday morning, I am a ball of nervous energy. Macy had sent me a million texts and social media posts wondering who I was. Who the mystery girl that Ason Antoni is with, really was. It was almost insulting that so many didn't even know my name. We have gone to school since pre-school, but I was never on their radar until now.

Until Ason noticed me.

I wasn't sure to expect once I arrived at school and that left a very unsettling feeling in my stomach. I couldn't eat my breakfast that the chef had prepared. Instead, I took an extra-long, hot shower and put a little extra time into my hair. After curling my hair and feeling unsatisfied with it, I ended up pulling my hair into a high pony-tail.

As I drive to school, my phone beeps and a text comes through the interior radio.

Ason: Meet me in the parking lot

Even though I'm alone, I smile like a giddy school girl at the text. Ason and I were developing into something more than just two people into one another. Our conversations were heavy and our make-out sessions were heavy.

When I pulled into the parking lot, I spotted Ason standing outside of his sleek car waiting for me. His muscular arms were crossed over his broad chest. His standard uniform blazer was hung over one shoulder and I swear he looked delicious as hell as he spotted me. I pulled in next to his car and people stared as they made their way through the parking lot.

Even as I exited my vehicle, I could hear their whispers and questions. Holding my head high, I tried to ignore their stares and judgmental voices. Ason rounds his car and saunters over to me. The heat of his gaze on me as my body heating. The glares from the girls around us causes a slight panic to rise in me, but Ason's smile somehow calms me down.

"Good morning," he greets me, moving to stand in front of me.

He blocks out the rest of the world and I am grateful for what he is doing.

"Morning," I say, my giddy smile causing me to blush.

Taking my hand, Ason looks into my eyes. "Get your stuff, we are walking in together," he orders.

"Today?" I ask.

It shouldn't be such a strange request, but I haven't really had time to prepare myself for this moment. I mean, people making assumptions about us is one thing. But to prove their speculations true...this feels huge.

"Yes. I told you that I wanted you. It's time for everyone to know that you are mine. That you are off limits," he states flatly.

Ason reaches around me, his lips lightly brushing my cheek as he reaches into my car and grabs my backpack. Slinging it over his shoulder, he pulls me as we start to walk across the parking lot. I'm left speechless.

Now, the world around us is set ablaze as all eyes are on us. All I can do is stare forward as we walk into school, hand-in-hand. The halls were filled and noisy, but once we enter, everyone goes silent. In all of the years that I've been around the Elites, I've never seen them enter the school without one another. Now, though, Ason is making a huge statement by walking in with me.

Macy is waiting for me at my locker and when she sees us, her eyes go large and a bright smile spreads over her features.

She offers a slight wave and wink and as she pushes off my locker and struts down the hallway.

Part of me wished that she would have waited for me or said something, but I knew she was enjoying this moment way too much. I would hear about this later; I knew for sure.

Micah, Talon, and Gabby rounded the corner and when they saw us, their eyes flickered wide for just a moment. The three of them nodded our way, but never approached us or said anything at all. Something told me that Ason had already informed his friends about what was going down today. Still, I doubt the rest of the school got the memo.

Stopping at my locker, Ason releases my hand and leans against the wall. "Are you ready for this?" he asks, smirking a little.

He seems to be enjoying my unease and I swat at him as I shove my books in my locker. "Well, I don't really have a choice now, do I?" I ask, playfully.

Leaning in, Ason places a kiss to my mouth. My knees almost buckle and my heart accelerates. "You definitely don't have a choice now. They all know that you are mine," he says, before placing one last kiss on my lips. "I'll see you later," he states, before winking and then walking away.

I'm left alone in the hallway, feeling as though I'm about to swim with the sharks alone.

By lunch, I feel like the entire school has heard about mine and Ason's relationship. Students who have never spoken to me before, have asked me questions like; how long this has been going on, was I new to the school, and if I had any gossip to share.

It had been exhausting avoiding their questions and comments, but somehow, I made it halfway through my day without incident. As I walked into the lunchroom, there was a different energy floating through the air. Everyone grew silent as I approached the salad bar, which was stationed next to the coffee bar. Macy was working on a group project in the library, so she wasn't there to save me now. Moving to order a salad, I heard someone say my name from behind.

Turning, I was shocked when I spotted Tara and an evil smirk on her face.

"Scarlette? Is that your name?" she asked coolly.

"Yes," I answered.

She had two friends beside her and they were narrowing their angry looking eyes at me, too.

"I hear things are hot and heavy between you and Ason," Tara announces loudly.

Her voice carries through the cafeteria and the few people who hadn't been paying attention to us, now were.

She laughs a little and places one hand on her hip. The other is holding an ice-coffee. I wish now, that I had noticed that small detail before.

"Umm..." I ramble on, unsure of how to respond. Without Ason with me, I'm not as confident.

"Well, I think it's time that you cool off," she yells out, throwing her full ice-coffee all over me.

Screaming, I jump back, knocking into a girl behind me who had just received her tray filled with a salad and drink. She stumbles and drops her tray, a loud bang radiating through the room.

"Look what you did," the girl screams out, throwing her hands up in the air.

Tears burn my eyes and my vision is blurry as I stare at the scene before me. The brown coffee drips off my white, button-down shirt and drenches my skirt and black ballerina shoes. The ice and coldness of the drink freezes my skin and all I can think about is getting out of here as quicky as I can. People start to laugh and point and just when I think it can't get any worse, Tara leans in and whispers in my ear, "Watch out, bitch. Ason is supposed to be mine. You are a nobody."

I can't take it anymore and I begin running, pushing past the people who have crowded around us, their phones out as they record the most embarrassing moment of my life.

As I sprint out of the cafeteria, the laughter and taunts follow me down the hallway. It's when I hear Ason's frantic voice calling after me that I finally break and fall to my knees in the middle of the hallway.

Chapter 22

Ason

Rage consumes me as I stalk toward the cafeteria.

Gabby had sent me a text message as Tara had started making fun of Scarlette. I refused to let Scarlette be ridiculed or hurt by anyone. That's why I had talked with Talon, Micah, and Gabby before school today. They knew that if anyone even dared to look at Scarlette, I wanted to know.

My family knew that bringing anyone into my life was serious. Not just because I had never cared to date before, but because our life was dangerous. Our fathers provided detailed security everywhere we went; including at school, but the risks were always there.

Now, as I barrel down the hallway, all I can think about is getting to Scarlette. When I make it to the cafeteria, I'm just in time to see Scarlette go running out of the wide, double doors. Tears stain her face and I don't think she even sees me as she rushes past. Her shirt is stained with coffee and the liquid drips off of her as she races away.

"Scarlette," I yell for her, but she doesn't stop.

I spot Tara and a group of her slutty friends and my rage only grows deeper. The entire cafeteria is laughing and talking about what just happened. Once I check on Scarlette, I will put everyone in this school in check. No one messes with the Elite and she is now one of us.

Racing toward Scarlette, I reach her as she crumbles to the ground. Quickly, I scoop her into my arms and as recognition crosses her features that I am holding her, she sobs even harder into my chest. Holding her tightly, I allow Scarlette to unleash her pain on me. If I could take it all away, I would.

After a few minutes, her crying starts to subside. "Tell me what happened," I demand, as I place my hand under her chin and force her to look up at me.

Her tear-stained face almost crushes me. An anger like I've never experienced before pulses through me knowing that someone hurt her this much.

She sniffles and I can see how difficult this is for her. "Tara poured coffee on me," she finally gets out.

Fucking, Tara.

I knew Tara had a crush on me, but I never thought she would go to such lengths to try and get me.

"I'm so sorry," I tell her. Shaking my head, I have to look away from Scarlette for a second in order to compose myself. "This is all my fault."

Scarlette's eyes go wide and then she places a soft hand on my cheek. The movement is genuine and comforting and I love how my heart swells from just her touch. "This isn't your fault. Tara did this on her own accord," she whispers.

A few students pass by us and I suddenly remember that we are sitting in the middle of the hallway. Though, I don't care. The whole world around us could blow up and I couldn't care less.

"She did it because of me. Everything around me is toxic. I'm unsafe," I say.

The words almost kill me to say. I feel myself returning to my old self. The guy who cared more about keeping Scarlette away from me, than chasing after her. But now that I have Scarlette, I just can't revert back to that guy. I care too much for her. Fuck, I love her and I won't let go of her now. Still, that voice in my head reminds me that I'm a monster—dangerous and lethal.

Scarlette stares deep into my eyes as though she is searching for something. "The only time I feel safe and happy is when I am with you," she says with so much conviction, I swear tears brim in my eyes.

No one has ever looked at me the way she is right now. Like I hang the fucking moon and she sees more in me than a rich prick with a tragic family. This look she is giving me and the soul piercing emotions radiating off of her is the reason why I would do anything for Scarlette.

"How can you feel so safe with me? I'm a monster."

I have to ask because I need one last confirmation that she sees something better inside of me. Maybe I'm searching for that or there is some strange desire harvested in me that needs her love and acceptance. Whatever it is, I wait on baited breath for her answer.

"I feel safe with you because I know that you would never let anything happen to me. You have a kind and gentle soul. Nothing about you is a monster," she says, sweetly. A smile appears and her tears see to disappear. "I was an absolute wreck until you came here and found me. Just having you hold me heals my wounds," she finishes.

Something stirs in me and suddenly, I am energized and determined more than ever to fix everything that has ever gone wrong for Scarlette. And damn it, I am going to start with the idiots here at this school.

Standing, I pull Scarlette up and hold tightly onto her hand. I begin to lead us toward the cafeteria again and I can already sense her unease as we approach the double doors.

"I need to go get cleaned up," she begins, but I stop her.

Shaking my head, I continue leading her. "No, I am going to let everyone know that this won't happen again," I rage. With my free hand, I text in my group chat for Gabby, Talon, and Micah to meet me back at the cafeteria.

As we walk into the cafeteria, a hush overtakes the room. All eyes are on us and Scarlette stands timidly next to me. I hate how intimated she is by the rest of the students here. We have all played a part in how she views herself and I refuse to put her back in the shadows again.

Jumping onto a chair, a few guys on the football team scoot back in their chairs as I move in front of them.

"What are you doing?" Scarlette hisses, as I release her hand and jump onto one of the lunch tables.

My black leather shoes stomp all over someone's burger and fries and everyone stares at me like I have lost my mind.

"Listen up everyone," I shout. I scan the crowd and spot Tara across the room, sitting with her cheerleader friends. Her mouth forms an O, and her eyes grow wide. Her friends all glance between her and me and they look just as startled and nervous as she does. Gabby, Talon, and Micah all stand beside me and form a circle around Scarlette. We are making a statement and it's a hell of a bold one. "Scarlette is now one of us," I yell, pointing to the rest of my group—The Elites. "Anyone who messes with her, will answer to me. Now, I believe someone was very confused earlier and threw some coffee on Scarlette. Only a dirty, pathetic, cunt would do such an immature thing. I mean, what girl can't get the hint that a guy doesn't want her? I guess I need to do this," I say, chuckling as I turn around and reach for Scarlette's hand.

She is baffled and shakes her head, no, as she nervously glances around the room. "Ason, you have lost our mind," she hisses.

Smiling down at her, I shake my head. "No, Scarlette. I haven't lost my mind. I have found my heart and soul." Turning back to the room, I watch their amazed faces as I continue. "I love Scarlette. If anyone even dares to look at her sideways, I promise, I will end you. Take that however you like," I deadpan.

Satisfied, I jump off the table and walk over to Scarlette. She still looks rattled as I grab her around the waist and pull her in for a deep kiss. A few people ooh and aww, while others turn away, clearly uncomfortable. I don't bother to check Tara's reaction. I made myself and clear and I meant every word I said. Anyone who hurts Scarlette will find out what the mafia can really do.

CHAPTER 23

SCARLETTE

"He told you that he loved you! In front of the entire school!" Macy squealed, as she ran up to my locker.

By the end of the day, everyone was talking about what happened at lunch. I was still in shock by it all.

Tara's attack.

Ason's declaration in front of everyone.

Telling me that he loved me.

Did I love him? Yes, I knew that I was in love with Ason, but this was all happening so fast.

"Keep your voice down," I chastised her.

"Are you serious? Everyone knows. You all are going viral," Macy cheers, shoving her phone in front of my face.

I watch as a video of Ason on the cafeteria table plays in front of me. Cringing, I hate how bewildered I look. My heart flutters as Ason's words ring through the air.

"This is all happening so fast," I tell her, grabbing my backpack and shutting my locker.

Ason has baseball practice this evening and I need to just go and relax. Something tells me though, that Macy isn't going to leave me alone.

"Scarlette, you deserve this. Enjoy every second of that glorious looking boy," she teases.

We walk out of the school as everyone smiles my way. I feel like I am in the Twilight Zone. No one has ever cared about me and now, I am the center of attention. I guess falling for the savage mafia boy has brought more changes to my life than I thought.

Over the next few weeks, my life has become a whirlwind.

The school has gone absolutely crazy over the news of mine and Ason's relationship. What is crazier, is how the girls can't seem to get over the fact that Ason finally has a girlfriend. The guy who was known for quick hook-ups and only one-night stands, now has a serious girlfriend. Some girls are rude and glare my way when Ason isn't looking. Others are overly nice to me in fear of what Gabby may do if they are caught doing anything but smiling at me. The attention I am receiving feels weird. Part of me misses when I was ignored and a nobody. However, I wouldn't trade anything for how Ason makes me feel because now, I feel alive.

Valued.

Important.

And those are feelings I don't want to lose.

Even his friends; The Elite, have warmed up to me. They weren't sure about me, an outsider, coming into their world, but with each day that passes, they are being nicer. Gabby even sat near me in class the other day! Then, Ason met my parents and I officially met his dad.

The world I have found myself thrust into is nothing like I expected. I wasn't sure what I imagined the mafia to be like, but from what I've seen, they are just a very tight-knit and close family. Images of Scarface and The Sopranos filtered through my mind and I was so nervous about being around all of the Elites and their infamous family members. I still hear the rumors of the Antoni Mafia Family, and I know Ason's fears about being a made man, but honestly, their world is kind of nice. I don't harp on what Aason's family name means because his story isn't about the mafia. It's about him and the man that he is on his own.

"Hey, beautiful," I hear from behind, as Ason's arms wrap around my waist.

"Hey," I say, turning in his arms so that we are now face-to-face. I throw my arms around his neck and pull him in for a kiss.

We are supposed to be having one of our tutoring sessions, but the last few times we have met here in our library conference room, not much studying has gone down. Instead, we spend our time devouring each other. Somehow, though, Ason has managed to get his grades back up. Things have been going great and even Tara has seemed to leave me alone. Though, her scowling continues, she hasn't tried anything on me again.

"I have a family meeting tonight, so I can't stay long," he drawls out, looking upset.

"It's ok, I have a paper to write anyway," I tell him.

A deep sigh escapes from him and something feels wrong in the moment. As I study him, I see his jaw tense and he looks stressed.

"Are you ok?" I ask, pulling back a little.

He runs a hand through his hair and looks away for a moment. "Yeah, I'm fine. I just have some things to talk to my dad about," he begins, but I still feel like there is something more.

I have learned with Ason that when he gets like this, not to push him. When he is ready to talk; he will. I guess that's why we have become so perfect together. Separately we are broken, but together we are perfectly imperfect. We complete one another and accept the other for who they are—faults and all.

"Will you call me later?" I ask.

"Of course, I will," Ason says, finally smiling.

I push him away and sit down in my chair. He flops down beside me and as we begin to try and get some studying done, neither one of us can help but to flirt with and touch the other. Our time together is precious and I know that these days are going to be forever implanted in my heart and mind.

Chapter 24

Ason

Sometimes, I feel like I don't belong in my world.

Staring around the large dining room table, I watch as all of the men talk with ease as they settle in for the meeting. Talon and Micah sit to on either side of me, while Gabby sits directly across from us. Gabby and her mother are the only two women at our meetings. In fact, they are the only women that I know of who are in the mafia and active with the dealings and business.

This meeting has been on my mind for a long time and I haven't wanted to tell Scarlette about it. She knows that I have to decide my future in the Antoni Mafia Family, but she doesn't know that the decision has to be made tonight.

Knowing my stress and reservations, my dad felt it was necessary to get me into the business early. As a senior, I will make my way in the mafia world in a few short months. Dread consumes me as I allow that notion to sink in.

"Ason, we are ready to begin," my father announces, as he takes his seat at the head of the table.

Swallowing, I steady my hands as I stare blankly back at him.

"Each of our children will one day step into the roles of their fathers and mother before them," he begins, nodding toward Micah, Talon, me, and then Gabby. "Ason, you will be eighteen next month, and that brings upon a very important right and transition in your life. As the heir to the Antoni Mafia Family Capo, you need to decide how you will rule this family. We have a job for you to do this weekend that will help solidify your place, because as you know, a made man must earn his way into the family."

My stomach churns and my palms become sweaty. I sense Gabby looking at me, but I don't dare move my eyes. As I listen to my father speak, a sickening feeling that I can't escape from nearly drowns me. The legacy my father is leaving to me is one that most men have and would kill for. It's a prestigious world where men rule and take drastic measures to ensure their power is never taken away. However, with each word he speaks, I feel as though I am falling into an endless black hole. I love my father and my family. I appreciate the lifestyle the mafia has afforded me, but I don't want to be a killer. I don't want my life to revolve around crime. I just want a chance to be normal. Without the weight of the world on my shoulders as I listen to the hushed whispers whenever I walk into a room.

"We have uncovered a spy who is working with a rival mafia family. We want you to go and kidnap him, then bring him here to us," dad says, as Solly, Chance, and Ryder all smile my way.

They, too, look proud and I can see the pride in my father's eyes glowing. Panic begins to take over and now my legs are shaking uncontrollably.

"Dude, what the hell is wrong with you?" Micah whispers next to me.

I can't speak or even turn to look at him.

"I can't do this," I quietly say.

Even as the words escape my mouth, I can't believe it was me who said them. Gabby's eyes go wide and Talon turns to face me.

"What did you say?" my dad asks in shock, as though he believes he didn't hear me correctly.

Shaking my head, I feel like I am going to vomit. The room begins to spin and air has long gone left my lungs.

I can't breathe.

I can't think straight.

Standing, I knock over the large, dining room chair and the bang against the hardwood floors rattles the China in the China cabinet. I hear gasps and shouting as I rush toward the French doors locking me inside this hell.

"Ason, what are you doing?" my dad shouts.

"Where the hell do you think you are going?" someone else roars, but I don't even look to see who it is.

I shove through the doors and as I make my way through the hall, my mom comes running out of the kitchen. Footsteps thunder behind me as my dad and I am assuming the rest of the men, come racing after me, too.

An arm reaches out and grabs me and I spin around, coming face-to-face with my dad. A look of shock covers his face and I know that what I am about to say will destroy him. But I have to say it.

"Dad, I don't want to be a killer. I don't want to be in the mafia," I declare.

Gasps, shouts, and cries, ring through the air. But what breaks my heart into a fucking million little pieces is the look of betrayal that is now painted across my father's face. He looks distraught and pained.

"Ason..." he begins, but I don't let him finish.

I know what this means. I could be cast out of my family. I could be killed. Left with no protection.

These thoughts have plagued me for months, but even though the risks are high they are risks that I am willing to take in order to find peace. I deserve this and Scarlette deserves to be with a guy who is happy. I turn around and look at him one more time and say," I'm sorry," before I rush up to my bedroom.

Slamming my bedroom door closed, I lock it and stand in the middle of the room, breathing heavily and shaking like a mad man. A blind rage spins inside of me until I am no longer able to take it any longer. My eyes scan the room, unsure of what I am looking for, until I spot my baseball bag in the corner of the room. Without thinking, I reach for my bat and begin swinging at everything in sight. I roar out a scream as my bat slams into the lamp on my bedside table. Glass shatters all around me and the sounds of the pieces hitting the wall and floor bring a sadistic smile to my face. My cold heart only freezes over more as I continue swinging the bat. I don't see the items I hit, I just feel the pressure and weight lifted out of my body. I don't stop until my arms can no longer hold up the bat. Collapsing onto the floor, I allow my emotions to break free and the world around me finally goes dark.

CHAPTER 25

SCARLETTE

Lying on my bed, music is lightly playing through my phone as Macy and I attempt to work on homework.

We've spent the majority of our time talking and chatting about Ason and how wild the school is reacting to our relationship. We ordered pizza and just talked. I was finally emerging from the shell I had hidden in over the years. I still wasn't overly social, but I was no longer the lonely girl who was afraid to be happy.

My phone began to ring and a giddy smile grew on my face.

"Oh, is that your new man?" Macy asked, laughing as she winked at me.

My heart began to flutter, but when I looked at my phone, it wasn't Ason's name I saw. It was an unknown number.

"Hello?" I asked, answering the call.

"Scarlette?" a female voice frantically asks.

The tone of her voice causes me to shoot up and my eyes go wide. "Yes, who is this?"

"This is Willow, Ason's mom. I'm so sorry to call you. I got your number from his phone..." she rambles on. I hear in her voice that she is on the verge of tears and my heart falls to the pits of my stomach. Something awful must have happened to Ason to make her sound so distraught.

"Where is Ason? Is he ok?" I ask rapidly.

"Ason is..." she pauses, and I wait, holding my breath for her answer.

Macy sits up, too, and mouths for me to tell her what is going on. I wave her away, only allowing myself to focus on Willow right now.

"Tell me that he is ok," I plead, tears now filling my eyes.

If something were to happen to Ason, I don't know what I would do. He is the first thing in my life to make me feel whole. Without him, my life would be nothing but darkness.

"Ason is ok. He got very upset tonight and I think you are the only one who can calm him down. I know it is very wrong of me to call you and worry you, but I didn't know what to do," she cries out.

My heart breaks for both Ason and his mother. I have no idea what happened, but for her to call me, it must be really bad. I know how the Antoni's are about their family affairs. Even I am left with only miniscule details most of the time.

I jump off my bed and begin frantically searching for my shoes. I need to go see him; to make sure he will be fine.

"I will be there in a few minutes," I tell her, and then end the call before she can protest.

Talking to Ason over the phone won't do any good. I need to see him in person. I need to hold him and remind him that everything will be alright.

"Scarlette, what is going on?" Macy asks me, as her worried expression stares at me.

"Ason is upset and I need to go be with him. I will tell you about it later, but I have to go now," I rush out.

Macy nods and follows me as I bound down the steps. Thankfully, my parents aren't home yet, so I don't have to answer any of their nagging questions.

Once I'm in my car, I speed through Savannah on my way to Ason's house. Each time I've been, Ason has driven, so I have to rely on my own memory to get me there. After only making one wrong turn, I get to his house in less than fifteen-minutes.

When I get there, the driveway is filled with luxurious cars and SUV's. The front door is wide open and I spot Willow instantly as she stands in the foyer, her hands to her mouth as she stares up toward the ceiling.

"Scarlette," she yells, as I run inside.

"Where is he?" I ask, not bothering with pleasantries.

"In his room, but Scarlette, please be careful. I've never seen him like this before," she whispers.

I can hear loud male voices somewhere down the hall, but I don't pay them any attention. I race up the stairs and pass Micah and Talon standing next to the top landing. They both eye me carefully, but neither dares to say a word. When I reach Ason's bedroom door, I feel a shift in the energy of the house. It's a mixture of anger and sadness and I hate how dark it makes me feel.

I lightly knock on the door, but there is no sound on the other side. Slowly turning the knob, it opens without resistance and I slip inside of his room. Instantly, I am consumed in darkness and as I take a step further inside, I hear the crunching of glass under my feet. Pausing, I pull out my phone and turn on my flashlight. What I see next frightens me to my very core. The room is destroyed. Holes in his walls, broken glass scattered all over the floor and furniture. Even some clothes are ripped to shreds. A baseball bat lay on his bed and I have no doubt that is the culprit.

Scanning the room, my heart shatters as I spot Ason lying on the floor. His eyes are closed and I rush to his side. His breathing is calm and steady; he is completely passed out. I'm sure he was overwhelmed with exhaustion after his tirade. Placing a soft kiss to his cheek, I realize that the last thing I need to do his wake him right now. He looks so peaceful so I don't want to ruin this moment. Biting my lip, I look around. Realizing I'm not leaving until he wakes up and we can talk, I decide to make myself useful and clean up his room.

I find a small trashcan in his En-suite bathroom and begin collecting all of the broken items. Glass, shards of wood, and things I have no clue what they go to are thrown away. Tears spring from my eyes with each item that I pick up and discard. For Ason to have this much rage inside of him means he was hurting far more than I ever imagined. All of these years, I thought that I was the one in pain because I felt ignored and neglected by my family. I wallowed in self-pity and doubt and made myself invisible at school. Refusing to allow myself to give in and have fun like a normal teenager. Now, I realize that my problems that once seemed so monumental, are tiny in comparison to what Ason is struggling with. He is faced with more challenges and decisions than I could ever imagine. He's living in a world that he can't ever escape from.

I must have been working for an hour when a deep voice startles me out of my own thoughts.

"Scarlette, what are you doing here?" Ason asks.

Spinning, I see Ason sitting up and rubbing his eyes. He looks disoriented and that only triggers more empathy and hurt for him.

"Ason, I needed to come and see you," I carefully say.

I have no idea what kind of mood he is in, so I am careful with how I approach him. Standing still, I wait for him to get up so I can better see him. Ason finally stands, and begins narrowing his gaze around the room. He moves to the wall and turns on the light. I've managed to clean up most of the mess, but now with the light on, I can see there are still pieces of debris that I missed.

His face is tomato red and his clothes are wrinkled and torn. I've never seen him look like this before. Damn, he is still sexy as hell.

The urge to go to him and hug him plagues me, but I still can't move. As though I'm frozen in place, I have to wait and see how he reacts to me being here.

"Scarlette, I never wanted you to see this side of me," he begins, his voice breaking. "I told you that I wasn't good enough for you. That the life I live isn't one I would ever want to put you in. Tonight, I just couldn't take it anymore. My rage took over and I destroyed everything," he said, tears now spilling from his eyes.

At the sight of seeing Ason cry, my body seems to unthaw and I close the space between us. I wrap my arms around his neck and pull him to me. At first, I feel him try to fight me, but soon he gives in and allows me to hold him like he has done for me so many times before. He feels like he destroyed everything and I know he means both figuratively and literally. I allow him to cry and unleash the pain, worries, and fear he has kept inside for far too long.

"Ason, I don't care what you did. All I care about is you." Reaching out, I caress his face and he looks up at me. "I don't care who your family is. You are enough for me because I love you," I say, before placing a soft kiss to his lips.

Shaking his head, he looks at me in disbelief. "How can you still say that? After you cleaned up my mess? Saw me cry?" he asks.

My hand is still on his cheek as I smile at him. "Don't you see? There isn't anything you could do that would make me turn away from you. I need you and you need me. Together, we fix everything that is wrong in our worlds. Just talk to me. Let me help you," I plead.

Ason stares at me for what feels like forever. After a few minutes, he hugs me again. "I swear, I don't know why you love me, but I will spend the rest of my life proving to you that I am the man you think I am," he declares.

I have no idea how long we stand there holding on to one another, but it doesn't matter. I think Ason had to break to finally find a way to become whole again. He knows that he has me as his ally and nothing will ever change that.

Chapter 26

Ason

In one night, my entire life imploded.

I single-handedly destroyed my father's faith in me of ever taking over the Antoni Mafia Family. In all honesty, Talon or even Gabby would be a better fit, but I've never dared to say that to him. But now, I am faced with one of the biggest challenges of my life.

It's been two days since I blew up and wrecked my bedroom. My father hasn't spoken to me, my mother is watching me like a hawk, and Talon and Micah haven't answered my texts or calls. Gabby has come by to check on me, but she really hasn't said much to me. I know that she's disappointed in me, but out of everyone, she understands me the most. She knew I was hurting and now, she knows why.

Then, there's Scarlette.

My perfect, beautiful, and angel of a girlfriend. She's been a gift from the heavens to me. She checks on me each day and just knowing that I will see her face, has kept me sane throughout these tortuous days. I have to go back to school next week and begin preparing for graduation. But tonight, I have to meet with my father and the rest of the Antoni Mafia Family. My fate will be handed down to me and I have to accept whatever it is.

The heavy silence fills the room as we all gather around the dining room table.

The very same table that I sat at only two nights ago when I informed my family that I didn't want to be part of the world that they had given me.

No one looks me in the eye, and that stings. I'm already being treated differently and I hate feeling like I am about to lose the people closest to me.

I am shocked when my dad remains seated at the start of the meeting. Instead, my uncle Chance begins. "Thank you for meeting again. We have something that needs to be discussed and a vote much take place," he states firmly. All eyes are locked on Chance and the room goes even more tense. I feel like I am suffocating as I sit there, awaiting my sentencing. Finally looking at me, Chance nods as he continues. "Ason, you have made a decision about your place in the Antoni Mafia Family. As a blood member of the mafia, you have provided us with a large obstacle. We will need to discuss the next steps," he says somberly.

Tears fill Gabby's eyes and I watch as she carefully dabs them away. Micah swallows hard and Talon glances my way briefly. I hate this so much, but now, there isn't anything I can do about it.

"Stop!" my father shouts, standing and slamming his hands on the large table.

Everyone jumps and a nervous energy fills me.

"I need to talk to my son. Alone," he roars out.

At once, everyone scatters out of the room. When the Capo makes an announcement, you do as your told.

Fear pricks at me as I watch my father stare me down. There is a mix of anger and sadness in his eyes and I've never seen him look like this before. When we are finally alone, he lets his shoulders drop and releases a heavy breath.

"Ason, I am truly at a loss for words right now," he begins, hanging his head low.

My father, who is one of the strongest men that I know, looks defeated and broken. I wasn't prepared to see my father like this. It is almost killing me. I've waited my entire life to tell him what I am about to say. Years of emotions are finally breaking the surface.

"Dad, I'm sorry that I have disappointed you. I appreciate everything the mafia has done for me, but I just don't think a life of crime is right for me. I can't kill. I can't hurt people," I confess.

I hear the irony in my words. I have a temper; just like my mother. But I've never intentionally hurt anyone before.

Shaking his head, my dad rounds the table and I instinctively take a step back. I've never feared my dad hurting me, but in this moment, I have no idea what to expect. When he sees me move, his eyes shoot up in shock.

"Son, I don't want you to ever fear me. I love you and I just want you to have the best life. The life you want. I am not going to lie and say that it doesn't hurt to know that you don't want a part in the mafia. It kills me, but I love you enough to let you make your own decisions. But please, let me help you," he pleads.

I don't expect any of this. I thought my father would disown me. Tell me he doesn't love me anymore. Instead, he wants to help me! Maybe Scarlette was right; things in my life are changing because I am opening myself up to having more.

"I respect the mafia. I just don't want to hurt people," I tell him.

"There is more to the mafia than killing," my dad chuckles. "You could own a business, become a doctor, an accountant, an attorney... the possibilities are endless. My companies will be yours one day. The Antoni Mafia Family will be yours, too, if you want it. Or, you can share the role and delegate it out to those you deem fit. You could be in control of everything. And, I want to clarify something. I've never killed an innocent man. I only go after those who have hurt or tried to hurt those I love. I need you to understand that, Ason. There are many sides to the mafia, but the Antoni's are on the good side."

I allow his words to sink in. I guess I've never really taken the chance to understand the inner workings of the Antoni Mafia. I allowed the gun shots I heard late at night and stories filled with heated murders to form my view of the mafia. When, in reality, there is more to it. Ryder and Chance own businesses. Solly and Gia train the new recruits. My dad owns businesses and helps protect local companies against rival mafia families. While I still don't want to ever be fully immersed in the life, I could play a role in keeping it a respected business centered world.

"Dad, I didn't realize how different everything was. I still don't know exactly what I want to do, but I do know that I could see myself helping out with the Antoni Mafia one day. Maybe," I explain.

A light sparks in my dad's eyes and that brings a sense of hope to me. While neither of us are ok with any of this, at least for now, we have come to an agreement that we both can live with.

Placing a hand on my shoulder, my dad pulls me in for a hug. It's nice and comforting as he holds me tightly. At some point, my mom sneaks into the room and joins our hug. After a few minutes, we separate.

"Is everything ok now?" mom asks.

I know she has been a wreck over all of this. Bringing her comfort now makes me happy.

"Yes," I tell her.

"So, are you going to tell me about Scarlette?" dad asks me.

I feel my heart race at the mention of her name. I am not even sure how to explain my love for Scarlette. Nodding, a wide grin appears over my face. "Yes, but I think I need to invite a few more people into this conversation." Stopping, I pull out my phone and send a text to my group chat. In seconds, Talon, Micah, and Gabby appear in the dining room with us.

We all sit down and for the next hour, I tell them all about Scarlette; the beautiful girl who stole my heart and changed my life forever.

CHAPTER 27

SCARLETTE

High school for me has been uneventful—until my senior year.

If you had told me years ago that my senior year of high school would be filled with a gorgeous boyfriend and a new outlook on life; I wouldn't have believed you.

In fact, I would have thought you were insane. But now, my life has evolved into one that I am proud to call my own. I have a boyfriend who loves me, new friends, and a hopeful future.

"Scarlette, what do you think of this one?" Macy asks, as she twirls in front of the full-length mirror.

To add more change to my already evolving life, I am now shopping for prom dresses with Macy. Yes, something I actually agreed to do!

The dress is ivory and molds to her frame perfectly. She looks stunning and I can't believe she found such a perfect dress.

"Wow, you look beautiful!" I admire, smiling back at my best friend.

Macy has been there for me in more ways than she can ever imagine. Being my only friend for years, she put up with my awkwardness and inability to be social. She loved me despite everything that I hated about myself and when I fell for Ason, she didn't judge me for going after one of the most dangerous boys in school.

"Thank you, I really like it," she gushes. Glancing back at me, she begins clapping. "Get in that dressing room and let me see your dress," she chastises playfully.

I scurry into the dressing room, laughing at my silly best friend. I try on the dress and when I emerge back into the small waiting area, Macy's eyes go wide.

"Is it ok?" I ask, as I make my way over to the large mirror.

I stare at my reflection and find myself smiling. The crimson red gown is fitting and hangs nicely on my body. A slit runs up to my thigh and the thin straps crisscross around my neck. I almost don't recognize myself; I look so different.

"Scarlette, you look fantastic!" Macy shouts, causing me to blush. "Ason is going to go nuts when he sees you," she says.

My heart leaps in my chest at the mention of Ason. I hope that is a feeling that never goes away. Just the thought of him has my body going into overdrive.

"I think this is the one," I say, spinning around for her.

After everything that has happened this year, going to prom with Ason will be the highlight of my life. He asked me the day after he told his father about not wanting to be a capo in the mafia. While I still don't fully understand the mafia lifestyle, I know enough to know that Ason's fears and trepidations were justified. I also know that his father's love for him runs far deeper than any rules of the mafia.

We change back into our normal clothes, buy our dresses, and then make our way back to my house. On the way, I get a text from Ason. He's having a bonfire tonight and wants me to invite, Macy, too. I think Ason told me that Talon has a crush on Macy and now that it is accepted that Ason is dating me, Talon feels like he can also date someone outside of their world, too.

Two hours later, we are sitting around a large bonfire.

Nestling in Ason's arms, we laugh as all of our friends share stories and talk about our upcoming summer plans. We find out next week if we were accepted into our colleges of choice and Ason and I both hope to go to Emory University in Atlanta.

"Scarlette, how does it feel dating a guy in the mafia?" Micah asks, taking a sip of his beer.

I feel Ason's arms tense around me, but I only hold on to him tighter. It is still a sore subject with Ason, but he's working through his anger issues and has even started seeing a therapist. A therapist who works only with the mafia so everything remains confidential...or else. Both Ason and I have grown so much, but we still have a long way to go before we are where we both need to be. But together, we will get there.

"I love dating Ason," I say, leaning back and placing a soft kiss to his lips.

Micah rolls his eyes and chuckles while Macy smiles and giggles. She's sitting next to Talon and he is looking at her with puppy-dog eyes. Even Gabby is having a good time. Sometimes, she can be a little hard to read, but I have enjoyed getting to know her.

Sitting here under the stars, a blazing fire keeping us warm, and lots of love and laughter, is the only place I would ever want to be.

I have no idea what my future holds, but I am excited to see how each of us grows. The once savage boy who I fell in love with has now become my forever.

The End

He's wild and ruthless, but can she avoid the temptation?
A Royal Academy Novel
Ruthless Elites
Amazon Bestselling Author
M.A. LEE

AFTERWORD

Want More?

The Elites are just getting started causing drama and breaking hearts in Savannah. Check out Micah's wild and reckless story. Turn the page to get even more steamy titles by M.A. Lee.

About Author

M. A. Lee resides in a small Kentucky town and enjoys writing tales of romance that includes the bitter and sometimes ugly truth of love, angst, heartache, and desire that all come with falling in love.